THE TRO

Toni sat, not m been hurt and disappointed and she'd tried to go on, but suddenly she knew she couldn't.

"It's no good," she said to herself. "I can't go back to college and face all those people. I can't face Brandt and the women in the office. I've got to get away from here right now before anything else goes wrong."

She grabbed her jacket and ran out of the apartment, slamming the door behind her.

On Our Own

This is a brand new SWEET DREAMS mini-series created by bestselling SWEET DREAMS author Janet Quin-Harkin, and starring best friends Jill and Toni, whose exploits delighted readers of TEN BOY SUMMER and THE GREAT BOY CHASE.

Back from their whirlwind tour of Europe, there's lots of excitement in store for Jill and Toni as they set out to discover if there is life after high school.

Ask your bookseller for titles you have missed:

1. THE GRADUATES
2. THE TROUBLE WITH TONI

Coming soon:

3. OUT OF LOVE
4. OLD FRIENDS, NEW FRIENDS
5. GROWING PAINS
6. BEST FRIENDS FOREVER

On Our Own

THE TROUBLE WITH TONI

Janet Quin-Harkin

BANTAM BOOKS

TORONTO · NEW YORK · LONDON · SYDNEY · AUCKLAND

RL 6, IL age 11 and up

THE TROUBLE WITH TONI
A Bantam Book/February 1987

Cover photo by Pat Hill

ISBN 0-553-25724-2

Published simultaneously in the United States and Canada

Printed and bound in Great Britain by
Cox & Wyman Ltd., Reading

For my daughter, Jane, who also goes through life like a tornado!

ONE

The clock on the square, red-brick building was striking nine as a small figure in bright yellow overalls ran across the courtyard. Her blond curls were tossed every which way by the strong wind blowing in off the ocean, and she had to stop twice to pick up the pencils and papers that kept slipping from the huge pile of stuff she was carrying in her arms. Toni Redmond was late, as usual.

Toni always tried to be on time, but the hands on her watch seemed to jump forward mysteriously so that even when she started out ahead of schedule she arrived late. She had especially wanted to be on time today, since it was her very first day of college. Usually, with Toni, the first thing that went wrong triggered a second mishap, and then a third, until it was too late to repair the damage, and another Toni Redmond disaster had been born. She hoped today would be different. She didn't want to destroy her entire college career on the first day. Her best friend, Jill, was already writing for the newspaper at Rosemont College. Her column on freshman life

1

had made her a campus celebrity. Nearly everyone at Rosemont knew who Jill was. Toni wanted everyone at her college to know her, too.

Three months earlier, Toni and Jill had planned on being roommates at the state university. They had even begun to choose what posters to hang on their walls. Then Toni's father had been struck by a heart attack in July, and her family's life was changed overnight. Not only would her father be unable to return to his old job, but it would be some time before he could do any work at all. And his disability payments were a lot lower than his salary had been. Her mother, whose income from her artwork was never steady, had virtually halted her career to look after Toni's father full time. So Toni had agreed to live at home, postpone going to the university. Instead she would get a job and attend classes at the community college. In spite of their worries over Toni's father, her parents were both enthusiastic about her plans. They wanted her to do well enough at the community college to transfer to the university as soon as possible. She was determined not to let them down.

Still, Toni felt a little stab of fear every time she thought of her parents' expectations. At high school she hadn't been the world's greatest student. She had only survived because Jill had helped her through the horrors of math and chemistry. But she was determined to do well in college on her own, even with Jill a hundred miles away at Rosemont, where she had decided to go after Toni had announced her own change in plans. Toni was determined to take only serious courses and to come out with lots of useful skills and good grades.

The counselor at the college had been hesitant when he saw her proposed course load.

"This seems quite heavy for a first quarter," he'd said. "These are all demanding courses, and you say you're looking for a job, too. I don't want you to take on too much and then end up having to drop a course because you can't keep up with everything."

"But I need all these subjects," Toni had said. "I know I need the English, and the people at the employment agency said they could only get me a real office job if I had some business courses. That's why I'm taking business math and computer science. I don't want to earn the minimum wage all my life. I've got to save for my transfer to State U."

The counselor had smiled kindly. "You're a very ambitious young lady," he'd said. "And I wish you well. But remember, college is a time to experiment and try out new things—and have some fun, too."

"I am trying out new things," Toni had said. "I'm in an art course. I haven't taken art since I drew stick people in second grade. But my mother's an artist and I thought I might discover a hidden talent." She'd glanced down at her hands. "I must have one somewhere," she'd added in a small voice.

"I would guess that you have many talents," the counselor had said, leaning forward encouragingly in his chair. "Toni, what's your biggest dream for your future?"

Toni had shrugged her shoulders. "I used to think about being an actress," she'd said, blushing slightly. "But that seems impossible right now. I mean, I can't even think about a career like acting when my father is at home and may never work again. I've got to get practical skills like computers and things."

Toni forgot about the counselor as she ran up the steps of the fine arts building. She shivered, although the hallway inside the front doors was pleasantly warm. *This is dumb,* she thought. *I bet Jill sailed through her first classes. But then, she was taking English and history and things she knows she's good at. I might be just terrible at art and computer science. And as for business math . . .* The thought of business math made her feel hot and cold at the same time. But she had studied enough want ads to know that bookkeepers made a lot of money. So did computer operators and programmers. And making a lot of money as soon as possible was uppermost in her mind at the moment. In her current favorite daydream she saw herself arriving home from her first day at the office and walking into her parents' living room with a big bouquet of flowers for them. "You don't have to worry about money anymore," she was saying. "I'm making enough to pay all the bills!"

I'm hardly going to be hired for a high-powered job if I can't even find the art room on time, Toni thought in panic as she clattered up the stairs. The halls were all empty. Everyone else had apparently found their assigned rooms with no problem. As she hurried down the hall, she peered through windows to see students busy at metalwork and ceramics, painting and printmaking, but nowhere did she see anyone peacefully sitting and drawing fruit and flowers.

At first, Toni had planned to begin with sculpture. She'd wanted to discover if she had inherited any of her mother's talent. Before class registration, she'd sneaked down to her mother's studio one day and tried chipping away at a block of stone. "What do you think of it?" she'd asked her brother Will, who happened to be passing by the door. "Very realistic," he'd said. "But why would anyone want to make a sculpture of a lamb chop?"

"It's supposed to be a dolphin," she'd said angrily. She'd heard his laughter as she walked away.

Then Toni had decided that she should learn to draw first so that she would really understand what her subjects looked like. She had signed up for Life Drawing 1–2.

Finally, at the end of a long hall, Toni found a door with the words "Life Drawing" scribbled on binder paper taped to it. About thirty students were already busy sketching at easels. As she pushed the door open it squeaked loudly, making a lot of them look up. Toni managed a weak smile at the teacher. "I'm sorry I'm late," she whispered. "I didn't know where the fine arts building was." The instructor, whose unruly black hair and heavy-rimmed glasses made him look like a student himself, gave her an amused grin. "No big deal," he said. "We've just started. There are a couple of empty places at the back. Just move your easel to a spot where you can see. Your choice of technique today—any medium. Basically I just want to see what everyone can do."

His friendly smile made Toni relax. She walked to the back of the room and put her pad of newsprint on one of the free easels. Casually she glanced toward the people on either side of her. On one side several older women were all working hard. A cute guy stood on her other side. *Maybe I can ask him for help later,* she thought. Everyone was working so intensely Toni worried that they all had been art students for years.

Well, I'll show them I'm as professional as they are, she thought. She opened her bag and took out several pencils, a box of pastels, some charcoal, and erasers—all things her mother had pressed on her before she'd left. "The basic tools of drawing," her mother had called them. Toni selected a fairly soft pencil and looked up to see what kind of fruit she was supposed to be sketching. On the platform behind the teacher's desk stood a young, plump man, one foot resting on a low stool, one hand on his hip. His chest was bare—and so was the rest of his body.

"But that man's naked!" Toni exclaimed before she could stop herself. Heads whipped around to look at her. Some of the students giggled. Toni felt her cheeks turn crimson with embarrassment. *I must be in the wrong place*, she thought in panic. *How can all these people just sit there calmly drawing a man with no clothes on? This must be the advanced class or something. I've got to get out of here!*

She started to gather up her pencils and erasers again. Her trembling fingers knocked over the box of pastels, and it fell to the floor with a loud crash. Pieces of chalk rolled in all directions under people's feet. "Oh, no. I'm so sorry—excuse me," Toni muttered as she dropped to her knees and started to crawl among the tangle of legs, trying to gather up her pastels as quickly as possible. Her one thought was to grab her supplies, escape, and never be seen in the fine arts building again.

As she rose to her feet, her hands rainbow-decorated with pastel colors, she almost bumped into the instructor, who was standing beside her.

"What seems to be the problem?" he asked, still looking amused.

"Problem?" Toni squeaked. "Problem? I'm . . . I'm . . . in the wrong place. I've got to get out of here. I mean, I'm supposed to be drawing fruit or something. Not naked bodies."

The instructor laughed. "This is life drawing one–two. Where are you supposed to be?" he asked.

"This really is life drawing one–two?" Toni asked, her big blue eyes wide with surprise.

"What did you expect life drawing to be?" the instructor asked, reaching up to adjust his glasses.

"Drawing from life," Toni muttered. "Uh—I thought we'd start with easy things, like apples and chairs."

The instructor threw back his head and laughed loudly. "For future reference," he said gently, "life drawing means drawing the human body, and you can only learn how the human body really looks if you draw it unclothed. The model's not embarrassed. Why should you be? After all, you wouldn't expect to draw an apple wrapped in a paper towel to start with, would you? You only learn to draw apples by drawing them naked!"

Toni managed a weak smile in return. "I don't get embarrassed by naked apples," she said.

The instructor put a hand on her shoulder. "Are you a freshman?" he asked. Toni nodded. "And you want to learn to draw?" She nodded again.

"This is really an excellent beginner class," he said. "But if you feel you're not ready for it yet, then I might suggest trying introduction to drawing and painting over in room three fifteen. They really do start with pears and chairs."

Toni gathered the rest of her things together. "Thanks," she said, "I really think I'd be happier trying that right now."

"Maybe I'll see you next quarter," the instructor said. "After you've been out in the real world a little longer."

Toni nodded. "I'm beginning to feel like I'm not ready for the real world yet," she said.

"Give it a try," the instructor said. "It can be fun." Then he winked at her. It was a friendly wink, and Toni smiled to herself as she made her way toward room 315.

TWO

By the end of the first week of classes, Toni began to wonder whether the real world was going to be any fun at all. True, after the naked-model incident she hadn't made a fool of herself in any classes—except in computer science, that is. But that was a mistake anybody could have made. She'd been feeling very nervous about the computer class. Machines and Toni had never mixed very well in the past. Standing outside the door of the computer lab she'd recalled vividly how in third grade, she had managed to wind the school film projector backward, so that all the film got jammed around the outsides of the reels. She'd never been asked to be audio-visual monitor again the whole time she'd been in elementary school. Now here she was, about to face a computer. Her imagination leaped and she could almost hear the whispers: "That's the girl who single-handedly wiped out an entire program it took six months to compile—the girl who blew the fuse on a whole roomful of Apple Twos!"

Toni had glanced up nervously when a young man came to stand beside her at the computer room door. "Hi!" he'd said brightly. Having found herself surrounded by mostly older women in suits in her business math class, Toni had been delighted to see another student who wore blue jeans and a faded T-shirt.

"Hi!" she'd said hopefully. "You don't know how glad I am to see you. I thought I was the only student in this college under the age of sixty. Are you as terrified about this class as I am?"

The young man had grinned. "Are you terrified?" he'd asked. "You look pretty calm, cool, and collected to me."

"But I'm not," Toni had confessed. "I'm scared I'll be the only person in the room who doesn't know a ROM from a RAM, whatever they are! Don't you feel that way?"

The young man's grin had widened. "I hope not, for your sake," he'd said. "You see, I'm the instructor!"

"Oh, no," Toni had stammered. "I'm so sorry. I mean, it's just that you don't look like an instructor. Most instructors are—um—kind of old and distinguished looking."

"Sorry to disappoint you," he'd said. "But when you get to college there's no longer a hard-and-fast rule that the teachers have to be older than the students. Anyway, you don't have anything to be terrified about in this class. We start at the

11

beginning and go very slowly. We even cater to people with computer phobia."

"That's me," Toni had said.

"Nonsense," the man had said. "We'll have you speaking BASIC like a native in no time at all. What's your name?"

"Toni Redmond."

He'd stretched out his hand. "I'm Bill," he'd said. "We're going to have a great time together, Toni."

I wish Jill were here, Toni thought, for the hundredth time that week. Jill would have laughed with her about the art class, and Jill would have immediately understood the first pages of the computer manual, which made about as much sense to Toni as Chinese. She was still stuck on the first page, which began: "The command mode is for manipulating text . . ."

The other students seemed to understand the instructions, because they were already putting disks in their machines and responding to the words that appeared on their screens. Toni was still hesitant about manipulating text, whatever that meant! She had a sinking feeling that once she manipulated it, she might never be able to un-manipulate it.

As she trudged out of the computer lab on Friday, she thought she would give anything for the sight of a friendly face. So she was delighted when she heard her name being yelled across the courtyard:

"Toni! Toni Redmond!"

Toni spun around to see Alicia Alberti and Dina Davidson, two girls from her high school, waving at her. She'd never been very friendly with Alicia and Dina. They had belonged to the group who seemed to spend every waking moment on the fringes of the football team and had to be treated for cardiac arrest every time they broke a fingernail. In high school, she and Jill used to think they were pretty dumb. But now Toni was so delighted to see two familiar faces, she ran over to them.

"I couldn't believe it was really you," Alicia said. "Dina swore it was, but I was sure you'd gone to State U. with what's-her-name with the auburn hair."

"With Jill, right. That's what we were planning to do," Toni said. "But I had to change my plans because my dad got sick, and Jill ended up going to Rosemont."

"That brain school? Boy, what a snob," Dina said, tossing back her long, heavy hair. "I thought she was supposed to be your best friend."

"She's not a snob," Toni said sharply. "She would've been crazy to turn down a chance to go to Rosemont. It's one of the top colleges in the country. Besides, why should she hang around here, just because I can't go away to school?"

"But Rosemont sounds like the pits," Alicia said. "You have to spend all your time studying. I'll bet you anything we have much more fun here." She picked up her bookbag from a stone bench. "We're going over to the cafeteria. Want to join us?"

"Sure," Toni said, "I was beginning to think there wasn't anybody here I knew."

"But lots of kids from school are here," Dina said. "You remember Randy? He's here. And Zach and Tod. We have a blast together. . . . We all signed up for the same classes."

"You're lucky," Toni admitted. "I don't know what courses you're taking, but everyone in my classes seems to be over forty."

Dina threw Toni a sideways look. "You must have signed up for a lot of business junk," she said.

"I did," Toni admitted.

"What for? That stuff is so boring."

"I need to get a job," Toni admitted. "And somehow I don't see myself making a career out of working at McDonald's."

"Well, we all have to get a job someday," Alicia said, pushing open the cafeteria door and walking through ahead of them, "but I intend to put off that day as long as possible."

They made their way down the food line. Alicia and Dina each took a plate of cottage cheese and fruit. Toni chose the spaghetti and meatballs special and then added a piece of apple pie to her tray.

"So have you met any cute guys here yet?" Dina asked as she picked daintily at her cottage cheese.

"You mean who aren't over sixty?" Toni asked. "The only vaguely cute guy I've seen in a week is my instructor in computer lab. I was beginning to think there weren't any cute guys in this whole college."

Dina looked horrified. "Are you kidding? There are tons of them. Alicia and I signed up for flag football. That's sooo much fun, and we've already been to some cool parties . . ."

"And thrown some real fun parties, too," Alicia interrupted. "That one where the landlord threatened to throw us out at three A.M.—remember, Din?"

Toni looked from one to the other. "You've got your own apartment?" she asked.

"You bet," Dina said. "We couldn't wait to move away from home. There's five of us, just a couple of blocks away from here. It's great, Toni. Nobody bugging you all the time about when you're supposed to be home or go to bed . . ."

"My mom and I used to fight all the time," Alicia added. "She had this dumb idea that I had to be home by midnight every night."

"My folks were always getting on my case, too," Dina said. "Clean up your room, don't talk with your mouth full, don't say such rude things. . . . It was like being in the army or something. Are you still going through that Private Benjamin bit? It would drive me up the wall."

Toni smiled. "Oh, my parents aren't like that," she said. "I mean, they're really great. They pretty much let me do what I want . . ."

"You're lucky," Dina said. "But if you ever decide you want to move out, talk to us. We don't have any room in our place, but there's this big house next door—all studio apartments, and they always seem to have vacancies—at least, they always have this big sign up, right, Alicia? . . . And there are these two cute guys who live there."

"You mean the ones with the motorbike?" Alicia interrupted. "Boy, that blond one is a real hunk! You really should get your own place, Toni!"

Toni shrugged her shoulders. "I don't have enough money to pay rent, even if I did want to get away from home. How can you guys afford it, anyway?"

Alicia laughed. "Believe me, my mom would pay anything to get rid of me. . . . Anyway, the rent next door isn't so bad," she said. "You could afford it if you got a job."

On the bus going home Toni went over her conversation with Alicia and Dina at lunch. She couldn't help feeling a stab of jealousy that everyone she knew was now out on their own while she was still stuck at home.

I've got to stop thinking like that, she told herself severely. *I have the most wonderful parents. I'm so lucky . . . even if things at home are kind of strange right now. As soon as Dad gets better again, everything will be okay.*

THREE

"Is that you, Toni?" her mother's voice called as she let herself into the house.

"No, it's Tom Selleck, come to take you away from all this," Toni called back, dropping her bookbag in the front hall and pausing in front of the hall mirror to rearrange her curls. "Who else do you know who would let themselves in with a front-door key?" she asked, walking through the hall into the living room.

Two faces looked up expectantly from the afternoon newspaper.

"So how was your day?" her father asked.

"Fine, I guess," she said, walking past where they were sitting to sink down onto the chintz-covered sofa.

"Oh, that's good," her father said, beaming at her and nodding his head. "So everything's going well? You're getting something out of this college?"

"Sure, Dad," she said hesitantly, positioning a pillow at the small of her back.

"And the business math?" he asked, folding his section of the paper and placing it in his lap, as if he were preparing for a long interrogation session. "Is that still giving you problems?"

"Because if it is," her mother chimed in, folding up her section of the paper as well, "you can always come to your father for help, you know. He understands all those percentages and debits and credits and things, don't you, honey?"

Toni watched her father as he nodded. *He looks like one of those toys you see in the back windows of cars,* she thought. *Those furry little dogs whose heads go up and down . . .*

"You know you can always come to me, Toni," he said.

"Thanks, Dad," she muttered.

"Because it's so important to us that you do well. We don't want you to miss out on anything just because of my heart problem. We're really proud of you . . . the way you kept things going at home when your mother was at the hospital with me. . . . So anything we can do to help, you just give a holler, understand?"

"Sure, Dad."

Her father clapped his hands suddenly, making her jump. "And I bet you're starving, aren't you?" he asked. "I know when I was your age I was a bottomless pit. Your mother's made this wonderful soup from scratch."

Toni looked at her mother in amazement. "You made soup?" she asked.

"Don't look so surprised," her mother said, smiling. "I've always been able to cook, when I've had to, that is." Her eyes rested on her husband, seated in his chair.

"You should try the soup," her father persisted. "It has all the ingredients my doctor recommended for me . . . and it's delicious. Go ahead, get her a bowl, Margaret."

Toni didn't have the heart to tell them that she'd eaten a large plate of spaghetti only two hours earlier. She forced herself to smile and spooned her way through a bowl of floating carrots and other pale vegetables. She was very conscious of her parents sitting there, watching her every mouthful.

"Have you done any more on your Creation sculpture, Mom?" she asked, trying to divert attention from herself.

"I can't go down to the studio right now, dear," her mother said sweetly. "I don't want to be too far away from your father, in case he needs me."

"You should rig a telephone line down to your studio, then you could get back to work," Toni suggested. "Maybe Dad could help you figure out how to do it."

"Later, perhaps," her mother said hesitantly, "but right now I don't want him to do any rigging up of anything."

"What are the other students like?" her father asked, breaking a silence during which Toni was trying not to slurp her soup. "Made any new friends yet?"

"Oh, Arthur. Give her a chance," her mother interrupted. "She's only been there a week."

"Well, Toni's such a friendly girl. She usually gets to know people right away. Especially boys, right, Toni?" he teased, giving her a wink.

"I haven't met anyone yet," she said, wiping chicken broth from her chin. "I've talked to a bunch of people, but there doesn't seem to be anyone yet who . . ."

"Still missing Jill, I'll bet," he interrupted. "You two were so thick all those years. It's going to take time . . ."

"Oh, speaking of Jill," her mother said, jumping up. "I almost forgot. You got another letter from her today. She's very good about writing, isn't she?" She walked through to the kitchen and came back with a fat envelope. "Here you are, dear," she said, handing it to Toni.

Toni took the letter. "I'll read it up in my room, okay?" she said.

"Of course, Toni," her mother agreed. "You take a little rest, too. New experiences are very tiring. And I'll get started on dinner. We're having chicken breasts—will that be enough for you, or would you rather have one of those steaks from the freezer?"

"No, no. Chicken's fine," Toni called out behind her as she ran up the stairs two at a time.

When she closed the door behind her, she gave a big sigh. She looked at the envelope in her hands, turning it over and over as if that might be a magic way of bringing the person who wrote it to life. "Why do you have to be so far away, Jill," she whispered. "I miss you so much."

"She threw herself down on her bed and began to read.

Dear Toni,

    All is going well here. I think I can finally say that I've settled in at Rosemont. I really like having Cassandra as a roommate. She's so funny, Toni. She has this dry sense of humor and she can really put down obnoxious people. Our cat, Jelly Bean, is getting bigger and fatter every day because everybody else in the house sneaks her in goodies to eat—even our housemother, who's supposed to forbid pets. I really like living in McGregor. I'm so glad I was put here and not in Phillips or Hollister. All the with-it rich kids want to live in Phillips and all the brains are in Hollister, so we're the only normal human beings.

    Toni, I'm actually making friends. People come down to our room now and just sit and talk. You remember the two guys I mentioned to you who live in our house—

freshmen named Jason and Robert. They're really nice. I eat with them most of the time in the cafeteria. Guess what? Robert told us one evening that he went through the first weeks of college thinking he was the only kid who didn't fit in at Rosemont. Then it turned out that everyone else in the room had gone around thinking the same thing. We all came from normal, ordinary families and thought that the rest of the kids were rich! We laughed about that a lot. Maybe it's the rich kids who are the minority.

Robert is very easy to talk to. Jason is nice too, but he's sort of shy around girls. But Robert and I both have the same English teacher and we often talk about stuff we have to write for English assignments. In case you're thinking what you usually start thinking when I mention a boy, let me tell you that he has a girl friend at Lewis and Clark college and he knows all about Craig. In fact we play "Dear Abby" with each other about the problems of long-distance romances.

Oh, and speaking of romances . . . there's another boy in the house—Charles. I think I told you about him, too. He's the one that Sheridan and her crowd wanted to play a trick on. They wanted me to keep him talking while they filled his bed with soap flakes. Of course I wouldn't cooperate, so they all told me I was a jerk. Anyway, after that I tried extra hard to be nice to Charles. He's one of those people that other people like to pick on—obviously brilliant, but not very good in the people-skills department! Well, now I'm afraid I've been too nice to him, because he hangs around me whenever he gets a chance. He's nice enough, but definitely weird! I might need your advice on how to get rid of him without hurting his feelings. I know you're an expert on things like that.

How is your father doing? I hope he's up and around again now. Will he be able to go back to work? I'm planning to come home for the weekend in two weeks. I'm dying to see you again, also to see Craig. He's arranging to come home for the same weekend. Won't that be wonderful? I've hardly been in touch with him at all since we both went off in different directions. I've spoken to him on the phone a few times, but his frat house is always so noisy.

I'd better go—Robert is standing outside my window making faces at me and waving an English paper we have to write before tomorrow . . . sorry, Robert is now jumping up and down. I'd better go before they take him away in a straitjacket! Please write me soon and let me know how school and your job search are going.

Love, Jill.

Toni finished the letter and sat up on her bed, staring out into the backyard. A few twisted brown leaves still clung to the Japanese maple tree, but a carpet of red covered the lawn. One brave chrysanthemum drooped at a weird angle, but otherwise the flower beds were full of dead stalks. Nobody had had any time to look after a garden this fall. It was a sad scene, and it matched Toni's mood.

Jill's so lucky, she thought. *She's settled in and made a whole lot of friends. Maybe before long she'll forget about me and I'll just be left alone here with my mother and father hovering over me and nobody to talk to . . .* She had a sudden urge to write a long letter back, even though she might be seeing Jill very soon. She walked over to her desk and came back with a pad of writing paper.

"Dear Jill," she wrote.

Please don't die of shock at getting three letters from me in one year. I feel like I need to talk to someone right now and there's nobody else I can tell things to. I'm glad everything is going so well for you and that you're making friends. I can't tell you too much about college yet because it's all so new. The English is easy—just reviewing what we learned in high school. Business math and the computers are still a total mystery to me. Almost everyone else in those classes is older and already working. There are terrifying lady attorneys who want to computerize their offices and women who have been bookkeepers for years and want to brush up their skills. So the teachers take it for granted that everyone understands when they talk about cash flow and megabytes and other things I'd never heard of. I don't want to sound like an idiot, so I keep quiet. Do you know what pops into my mind every time the teacher says "cash flow"? A picture of an enormous bag stuffed with gold coins that pour out constantly. Wrong, right? Well I'm hoping to find a friend who'll help me keep up the way you used to. You know how I never could get the hang of percentages? Now, I have to do them all the time!

I'm slightly more hopeful about computers. First of all, the instructor is nice. He's young and wears jeans and T-shirts—also I think he likes me! Being irresistibly sexy and good-looking does have its advantages, you know!!

So I think I may survive in college, if I can just stand it at home. You're in for a big shock when you see my parents. You'll hardly recognize them, they've changed so much. You remember how my mother used to be lost for days down in her studio and wherever you looked in the house there were clay smudges? And you remember how on weekends my father used to sit and watch TV—when he wasn't working in the backyard—and never said a word to anybody? Boy, those seem like the good old days right now.

My father now spends all day, every day, in the armchair. His doctor told him he has to take it easy, and he sure is. He's so scared to try anything new. Sometimes I wonder if he'll ever go back to work again. Mom fusses over him all day. She hasn't been down to her studio since his heart attack; she won't leave him in case he should need her while she's in the basement. And she's actually cooking every meal! Imagine *real* food in our house, food that didn't come out of a can. Actually it's pretty disgusting, because it has to be low cal and low sodium and low everything for my father's heart diet, but Mom spends half the day preparing the junk.

The other half of the day they both spend fussing over me. I know that they feel guilty because I couldn't go away to college, but they've gone overboard, Jill. They just sit there, watching me, asking me questions until I want to scream. I know your mother would never let you leave the house in wet weather without your raincoat, but my mother barely even noticed if I was home or not. We used to have a joke that the boys could bring a friend to live with us for three years before my mother would discover he wasn't one of her sons!

I'd rather have it that way. I was looking forward to being away at school. I really need to be free, just like you are. I met some girls from high school today—remember Dina and Alicia who were cheerleaders?—and they already have their own apartment. They tried to persuade me to move in next door. I told them I had no reason to leave home, but the more I think about it, the better it sounds. Just to be able to make my own decisions and come and go as I please . . . but, of course, there is the small matter of money. I can't afford anything until I get a real job. The college career center is useless. They only have the kinds of jobs you and I always got stuck in, minimum-wage stuff that doesn't lead anywhere. I'll go to a real employment agency and I'll be able to convince them I know more about mega-bytes and cash flows than I really do.

Maybe by the time you come up for your weekend I'll have some good news at last. There must be a job somewhere that is crying out for a gorgeous, talented eighteen-year-old with no skills whatsoever. I'm dying to see you again—if you can spare me a moment away from Craig!

Luv, luv, luv, Toni.

FOUR

By four o'clock on the following Friday afternoon, Toni was about as depressed as she'd felt in her whole life. She'd been to four employment agencies. At the first one she'd failed the typing test because she'd spent half of the one-minute test time frantically searching for the on/off switch of the electric typewriter. At the second agency she'd been given a business math test—all on percentages. She made twenty percent of eight dollars come to a hundred and sixty dollars. The woman giving the test had laughed out loud. "I don't think any company would be willing to trust you with their accounts," she'd said. "They'd be bankrupt in a couple of weeks if you gave away a hundred and sixty dollars every time you took in eight!"

"You made me nervous," Toni had answered angrily. She hated to be laughed at, especially by a woman in a charcoal gray suit, with long red fingernails. "You were standing right over me. I only missed on the decimal point, didn't I?"

"You'd be surprised how much damage a decimal point can do," the woman had said, drumming her long red fingernails on the desk as if she couldn't wait for Toni to leave. "I suggest you pass your business math classes before you try for this sort of job again."

The interviewer at the third agency had made it very clear that the agency wouldn't send anybody out on a job interview unless that person had actually held down an identical job in the city for at least two years. When Toni had asked her what they planned to do when all the people who already had experience died of old age and there was nobody left to take their places, she hadn't even smiled in reply.

The interviewer at the last agency, Flying Fingers Secretarial Services, only wanted to talk about computers. He was a tall, slim man with a droopy mustache, wearing a pink shirt. He had greeted her with a smarmy smile, a casual wave, and a big, "Well, hello there!" Toni had decided on the spot that she disliked him.

"We are fully computerized, aren't we, dear?" the man had asked her, still smiling his smarmy smile. "Because computers are where it's at these days. Computers are what's happening."

Toni had glanced down at her hands, as if expecting to see wires shooting out of them. "We hope to be fully computerized soon," she'd said.

The smile had faded. "Then we had better come back again when we are, hadn't we?" he'd said. "Flying Fingers Secretarial Services does not send out half-trained people. We pride ourselves on our fully computerized people. Fully computerized people—they're where it's at these days . . ."

Toni had gotten up. "Oh, I can tell that," she'd said sweetly. "I mean, I could tell you were only a robot the moment I walked in." Then she'd stalked out without looking back.

That had been her one satisfying moment of the day, but it obviously hadn't brought her any nearer to finding a job. Visions of a year ahead, living at home, working part-time in Burger King, flashed before her eyes. *I know I could do lots of jobs well if they'd just give me a chance,* she thought. But it didn't look as though anybody was prepared to give her that chance.

She bought an evening paper and sat down on a stone bench in a downtown square. Rush hour was just beginning. People hurried out of office buildings and began lining up at stops. Toni watched them with annoyance. Why did they all have to look so efficient and professional and grown-up? Surely those women in the dark suits, with neatly permed hair, must once have started off as girls with unruly hair like Toni's? How had they gotten their first jobs? Had some employer in one of those tall concrete blocks that sprouted in the center of Seattle been willing to take them on when they were only partly computerized?

Toni shivered as she huddled on the bench. The wind whipped at her newspaper. Out beyond the white-capped water of Puget Sound she could see the distant peaks of the Cascade Mountains. Usually these majestic mountains were her favorite sight—apart from a roomful of boys or a Big Mac with catsup—but tonight they looked as grim and forbidding as the concrete towers looming around her. *I don't belong here*, something inside her whispered. *I'm just not cut out to be a businesswoman.*

She opened her paper and started to read through the want ads. There were pages and pages of them, all requesting "experienced" this and "highly qualified" that. Her eye skipped down the page, digesting the jobs one by one. Longshoremen wanted . . . There was a sexist ad if she'd ever seen one! It should have read Longshorepersons. Toni was tempted to go along and apply, just to prove that longshorewomen should be given a chance. A picture floated before her eyes of herself hefting huge crates, hooking them onto a crane . . . then she remembered all the things she had spilled and knocked over in her life. She visualized three million apples rolling down the Seattle waterfront. . . . *Maybe not*, she decided.

The only jobs requiring no previous experience seemed to be telephone surveyors, encyclopedia salespeople, and dishwashers. Then suddenly an ad caught her eye: THEATER ALLIANCE SEEKS FANTASTIC PART-TIME PERSON FRIDAY. Toni felt her heart beating fast. She knew all about the Theater Alliance. It was the top amateur theater group in the area. Sometimes they even hired professional actors to play leads. Theater Alliance productions always got rave reviews. Toni had seen their summer musical in the park, and it had been wonderful. Even as she read the ad she knew that, deep in her heart, she'd always dreamed of working in the theater. She knew that she never wanted to be one of those terrifying women who'd passed her, clutching briefcases, all most definitely fully computerized.

To work in a theater, she thought, her eyes shining. *What could be more perfect?* She let her imagination wander and saw herself walking behind the director, taking notes, ordering costumes, designing posters, being backstage during performances, and maybe one day being onstage acting. . . . "Our own Toni Redmond," people would say. "A star was right under our noses and we never knew. I'm glad she could use us as a stepping-stone for a great future."

Toni jumped up. She forgot all about getting an ordinary job and making enough money to pay for four years of college. She didn't even care what the Theater Alliance paid. She had to have that job. She took one look at the line at the bus stop and started hurrying on foot in the direction of the Theater Alliance building.

This time I know it's going to go right, she kept on telling herself. *I was destined to get this job. After all, it said* person Friday, *and today's Friday! Oh, I know good things are going to start happening* . . . and she began to hum "Everything's Coming Up Roses" softly, which made a few commuters stop in their tracks and turn to watch her.

The Theater Alliance was housed in a tall, narrow brick building, an old, converted warehouse close to the waterfront. The theater itself had been created from what used to be the basement and first floors. Toni pushed her way past tourists and fresh-crab stands, savoring the fresh sea smell and the exciting bustle there always seemed to be in this area. The tall entrance doors at the front of the theater were locked. Posters plastered across them announced: Coming Shortly, *The Mermaid and the Millionaire*—a hilarious comedy fresh from Broadway.

Having rattled the doors furiously, knocked, and peeped in through the cracks, Toni realized that she wasn't going to get in through the front doors and went around to the side of the building. In a narrow alleyway, littered with garbage cans, empty bottles, and piles of drifting newspapers, she saw a flight of iron steps going up to a small, glass-fronted door. She climbed the steps, opened the door, and found herself facing an elevator. The elevator, standing open, had just two buttons on the inside wall: Up and Down. Since Down would only lead to the theater, she decided to press Up. Her heart was beating very fast, and she leaned against the back wall of the elevator to steady herself. The door closed very slowly, with a horrible squeaking sound, then the elevator shuddered and, with a deep grinding and rumbling, began to jerk upward. Immediately Toni was taken back to that elevator in France . . . the little French hotel where she and Jill had spent their first night away from home. The hotel had been dirty and rundown and the proprietor had been very bad-tempered, but staying there had been an exciting experience. She'd felt, as she went up in that French elevator for the first time, that she was truly living instead of existing, that she was in the middle of a real adventure.

She hadn't felt that way again since she'd come home and her father had been taken to the hospital. In fact, she'd managed to shut off most of her feelings; she knew that the moment she allowed herself to feel again, the fear and the disappointment might rush in and crush her. Now, suddenly, she began to feel alive again. That mixture of excitement and a delicious fear of the unknown made her pulse race. "There really is a future waiting for me somewhere," she whispered to herself.

With a terminal groan the elevator shuddered to a stop. Slowly the door creaked open. Toni stepped out into a long, dark hallway. She could hear the clattering of a typewriter coming from somewhere. As she approached one of the doors, a voice shouted, "Oh, damn!" Toni pushed the door open a crack to reveal one of the most untidy rooms she'd ever seen—making even her own bedroom look neat by comparison. There were three or four desks, all but buried under mounds of paper. Some of the papers had toppled off the desks and lay strewn over the floor. Sitting at the desk farthest from the door was a woman who looked completely out of place. She was around forty, beautiful, very expensively dressed, with sleek blond hair perfectly arranged. Toni was sure she'd seen her somewhere before. The woman looked up in alarm when Toni tapped on the partially opened door.

"You nearly made me jump out of my skin," she said accusingly in a rich, smooth voice. "What do you think you're doing here? There's nobody working in the theater tonight except me."

"I'm sorry," Toni said hesitantly. The woman, when angry, was rather terrifying. "I saw your ad in the paper. Is this the right place? I mean—it was the only door I could find open."

The woman's face softened into a smile. "The ad in the paper? My goodness, you were quick. It only ran for the first time tonight. I didn't expect any response until Monday at the earliest."

Toni grinned. "It said 'person Friday,' and I always like to obey instructions," she said.

The woman smiled and extended her hand. "You could be a godsend," she said. "I was getting to the final stages of desperation here. I never learned to type, and I'm convinced that this machine positively hates me. It keeps skipping lines every time I look away. I'm Mariette Thompson— director of the Theater Alliance."

Then Toni remembered where she'd seen the woman before. Her picture appeared regularly in the society pages: "Mr. and Mrs. Walter D. Thompson hosted the party for the President . . ." "Lovely socialite Mariette Thompson at a ball to raise money for famine-stricken children . . ." Toni stepped forward and grasped the extended hand, noting the three sparkling rings on her fingers. "Toni Redmond," she said. "I'm pleased to meet you."

"And I you, Miss Redmond," Mrs. Thompson said. "You've no idea *how* pleased I am to see you. As you can see, we're in dire need of office help. Our last girl quit in the summer, and we're all volunteers with absolutely no office experience. We've been trying to struggle through—to save the company some money, but it became very obvious that we need a professional to run things. You've done this sort of work before, I take it?"

"Not exactly," Toni said, wanting the job so badly that she had to stop herself from lying. "But I'm taking business courses in college right now . . ."

The smile faded from Mrs. Thompson's face. "Oh, then you mean you haven't actually had experience as a secretary?"

Toni shook her head. "But this is the kind of job I've been dying to get. I really love the theater."

"I'm sure you do," Mrs. Thompson said kindly. "But I'm afraid it wouldn't make sense for us to hire someone like you. You wouldn't be any improvement over the rest of us. We need someone with top office skills who can zoom through our correspondence, file everything neatly, answer phones, and get this office looking less like a garbage dump."

"But I could do all that," Toni said, "—if you'd give me a chance. I'm a good worker and I'm very quick."

"But the point is, you don't have any experience, do you, Miss Redmond?" Mrs. Thompson said, shaking her head so that her dangling gold earrings chimed like little bells. "I'm afraid we simply need someone with experience. But thank you for applying so quickly. . . . Now, if you'll excuse me, I have a stack of addresses to type for our mailing." She turned back to her typewriter and began pecking at the keys.

Toni stood there, fighting back her tears. It couldn't be all over—not as quickly as that. She couldn't just go and forget about the job. She wanted it so badly. . . . She didn't want to work in an ordinary office, full of computerized people— she wanted to work here, in a theater.

She took a deep breath and marched over to the desk. "Look, Mrs. Thompson . . ." she began.

The face this time was no longer kind. "I've said I was busy, Miss Redmond . . ."

Suddenly something inside Toni snapped. All those rejections—being polite to people who treated her as if she were some kind of nonperson exploded in her brain. "I won't go until you listen to me," she said angrily. "I'm beginning to wonder if people like you ever stop to think about what it's like to be a person like me. I want a job badly. I need to save money for college. I'm prepared to work very hard, and yet everywhere I go I hear the same thing: I need experience. Well, I'd like to know where I'm supposed to get this experience if nobody will ever give me a break. I may not have worked in an office, but I've done lots of things. I've worked around the theater in high school—I've built sets and made costumes and even had the lead in plays . . . and I've had to work very long hours as a waitress so I know I have enough energy, and I've even addressed thousands of envelopes by hand. You probably don't know what it's like to need a job— how *would* you know? And I bet you've never dreamed of getting a special job—not one that just pays you money, but one that makes you feel good when you come to work every day." Toni suddenly realized that she was yelling. Her voice echoed back to her along the long dark hallway. She stopped in embarrassment and looked down at Mrs. Thompson. "I'm sorry—I'd better go," she said.

But Mrs. Thompson did not look angry. Instead she had a strange, faraway look in her eyes. She folded her hands in her lap. "Don't go," she said. "I understand what you're saying. And, believe it or not, I do understand how you feel. I understand more than you will ever know. I wanted a special job once, too—when I came out of college. But I had very strict parents and very rich parents, who made it eminently clear that no daughter of theirs was going to work in a humble job. So I gave up my dream. I was a good daughter . . . and after that, a good wife . . ."

Mrs. Thompson pushed back in her swivel chair and stood up. She gazed into Toni's eyes. "But you—you're prepared to fight. I like that. I wish I'd fought a little harder." She toyed with the gold chain around her neck. "Look, Miss Redmond—or may I call you Toni?—I really can't promise you anything. But I'm willing to give you a try. I'll give you two weeks, just to see if you can do the job. How does that sound?"

Toni's eyes were shining. "That's great," she said. "I was only asking for a chance. You won't be sorry, Mrs. Thompson. I'll be the best worker, I promise."

Mrs. Thompson smiled. "I want you to realized that this is not a glamorous job," she said. "You won't be down there, onstage, getting the applause, you'll be working hard at all the unglamorous things that have to be done. And you'll often have to work very late. I'd like you to take tickets at the box office when a play is running—then count the money and deposit it each night. How would you handle getting home late like that? Do you have a long commute? What would your parents say about it?"

Right then Toni was prepared to say that her parents wouldn't mind if she went around the world in a leaky hot-air balloon. "Working late would suit me fine," she said. "And as for getting home late . . . I was planning to get an apartment closer in to town anyway."

Mrs. Thompson beamed. "That sounds splendid," she said. "Well, Toni, you can consider yourself hired for a trial period. You couldn't possibly start tomorrow, could you? I know it's Saturday, but we have got ourselves so behind . . ."

"I can be here," Toni said. "Thank you very much. I can't wait to start!" Then she turned to go.

"Watch out for our elevator!" Mrs. Thompson called after her. "It's very temperamental. Press the button gently or it may refuse to move."

Toni laughed. She laughed all the way down in the rattling contraption, and she shouted for joy as she leaped down the iron steps. Then she hummed another chorus of "Everything's Coming Up Roses," all the way to the bus stop.

FIVE

Dear Jill,

This letter is being written by a real office person. I was sitting at my typewriter, just about to go home for the day, when I decided to use my new secretarial skills to write to you. You should feel deeply honored, because my fingers are already tired from typing oodles of letters.

Anyway, I'm sure you're dying to know about my job—it's the job of my dreams, Jill. I'm working for the Theater Alliance . . . Remember when we went to see *Fiddler on the Roof* in the park that time? Not that I'm doing anything glamorous like acting, but here in the office I get to talk to theater people all the time, and that's wonderful. The other workers are all volunteer ladies. Mrs. Thompson, the woman who runs the Alliance, always appears in the social pages for doing good deeds, but she's really very nice. The other two are more my age, but are married already—I guess to rich husbands or they wouldn't be able to hang around here without getting paid.

Anyway, the ladies were very impressed by my efficiency. Actually I had to keep looking down at my typewriter to stop myself from laughing. . . . I mean, I felt as if I were acting the part of "efficient secretary!" Judy, she's small and dark, told me I was a genius, because I got things filed away, and Pam, who looks a little like you, brought in her two-year-old son. He crawled around her feet while we worked and I had to keep jumping up to stop him from putting horrible things in his mouth. His mother didn't seem to notice. I don't think the kid's going to make three if she doesn't wise up!!

I began to feel like an important person, not like a teenage klutz. . . . And I wasn't klutzy once all day. I didn't drop anything or break the copying machine, and I actually made coffee for everyone and nobody died of ptomaine poisoning! There's hope for me yet, Jill!

So I really think I'm going to like this job. Of course right now there's so much chaos in the office that I hardly know where to start and this is the time of year when they have their big season-ticket subscription drive, so we've got piles of letters waiting to be answered—not more envelopes, I hear you sighing—but it's going to be fun working here. The leading lady dropped in today—her name's Adriana—I bet that's not her real name. . . . She's playing the mermaid in the play that's coming up. She had locked her keys in her car and had to have me call the AAA for her—that sounds like something I would do, doesn't it? Maybe all of us creative people are the same! She was really sweet to me (if a bit too gushy). Hey, I might get to be buddy-buddy with the stars! Watch for my picture in the society columns!!!

So it really seems as if big things are happening to me. I may have something else to show you when you come up for the weekend. . . .

Toni stopped typing and looked out the window. The afternoon sun was painting a bright square on the wall behind her. The whole building was peaceful and quiet. *Should I go ahead and tell her about the apartment?* Toni wondered. *Not until I've really got it and I've told my parents about it*, she decided. She glanced down at her watch. *In half an hour I may have my own apartment*, she thought. It seemed too good to believe. Hurriedly she finished the letter.

Well, I'd better be going now. They've trusted me to lock up the office and I've got a million and one things to do before I go home this afternoon. I can't wait to see you again. I doubt if you'll recognize the smooth, sophisticated career woman that I am now!!!

Yours very truly,

Toni M. Redmond, Secretary

Toni pulled her letter to Jill out of the typewriter with a flourish, stuck it in an envelope, and locked up the office. "Apartment, here I come," she said as she bounded down the iron steps.

She's been thinking about a place of her own ever since her first conversation with Dina and Alicia. Then it had seemed so impossible, but in the week since then the idea had been growing. . . . She'd begun to think more and more that staying at home would only end up hurting the whole family in the long run. Toni had never been noted for her smooth temper, and the fact that she hadn't yet exploded was some kind of miracle. But it was taking a giant effort on her part not to explode with both her parents constantly fussing over her, treating her as if she were a fourth grader all over again.

The night before, she'd finally made up her mind to go. Getting a job, having enough money to support herself, and then declaring to Mrs. Thompson that she was planning to move closer in to the theater had almost made her decide to go ahead and start looking. Her parents' reaction to her job had been the final clincher . . .

She'd come home, bursting with excitement, expecting them to be as thrilled as she was. Instead her father had started fretting again.

"I really don't like the thought of you working downtown," he'd said. "That's not the safest part of town for a young girl—and coming home late at night on those unpredictable buses—! Couldn't you find a job closer to home?"

"But, Daddy, this is the job I really want," she'd pleaded. "There's nothing out here in the suburbs except McDonald's."

"Well, if this is what you really want . . ." he'd said, his voice trailing off as he looked out the window.

"It *is* what I really want," Toni had said, turning away to hide the hurt in her face. "I thought you'd be proud of me for getting a real job that could lead to good things . . ." Then she'd turned and stalked out of the room.

Afterward, as she was helping her mother clean up in the kitchen, Mrs. Redmond had said, "Don't be too upset by your father. He has nothing better to do than to worry about you right now. You take whatever job you want. He'll get over it. Just make sure you remember to phone and let us know what time you're coming home. . . . I don't want him pacing the floor all night worrying about you."

"But he never was like this before," Toni had said hopelessly. "I never had to tell you where I was every minute. You both trusted me."

"And we still do, honey," her mother had said. "It's just that your father has had his life thrown off balance. He was so strong and healthy, and suddenly he's become a helpless invalid. Now he realizes that life is full of things that can go wrong, and he can't help brooding about them."

"I know, but I just can't go on like this anymore—allowing myself to be treated like a little kid just so we don't upset Daddy," Toni had snapped, her self-control stretched to the breaking point. "All my friends are out on their own, living their own lives . . . I've given up the university for you but you can't expect me to give up my whole life."

"Of course we don't, Toni," her mother had said, also sharply. "Just try to be a little patient, until your father gets back on his feet."

"The way things are going, I sometimes wonder if that's ever going to happen," Toni had said bitterly.

"Toni!" her mother had said in a horrified voice. "What a terrible thing to say!"

"Well, it's true," Toni had snapped. "He's not even trying to help himself. He's convinced himself that he's an invalid and that he'll be one for the rest of his life. And all you ever do is fuss over him and make him think that getting out of that chair would be like the kiss of death!"

"He's had a heart attack, Toni. Don't you understand that?" her mother had said angrily.

47

"Of course I understand," Toni had said, "but I also understand that he's not going to recover unless he starts taking an interest in life again. I've read things about heart attacks—lots of patients started exercise programs almost immediately. They were out jogging at this stage—not sitting in a chair watching *The Days of Our Lives*."

"I'm surprised at you, Toni," her mother had said, turning away. "I didn't think you were so selfish—I thought you cared about your father."

"I do care," Toni had said, tears stinging her eyes. "That's why I want him to get better . . ."

Toni had been unable to hold back her tears any longer. She'd bolted from the kitchen and had run upstairs to her room. *I can't go on like this*, she'd thought. *I can't spend every minute worrying that just because I'm a few minutes late my father could have another heart attack . . .*

She'd swiped at her eyes and dialed Dina's number. Dina answered right away. "Uh, Dina"—Toni cleared her throat—"do you remember those apartments you were telling me about?"

"Yeah, sure," Dina had replied. "You want to rent one? Cool. But don't ask me to come with you," she'd said. "Old Mr. Paolini, who owns the building, is always complaining about the noise we make. He's called the police a couple of times. You might not get a room if he thought you were a friend of ours!"

As Toni walked in the direction of Dina's street, she felt excited and scared at the same time. This was one of the biggest steps she'd ever taken: she was going to be on her own. *I wish you were here, Jill,* she thought. *What if there aren't any vacancies? What if I can't afford the rent?*

The house, in a good location for Toni—within waking distance of the college and only five minutes by bus from her job—was on a quiet, tree-lined block just off a noisy, bustling thoroughfare. The block had obviously been very elegant at one time. The houses were three or four stories high with lots of carved wood decoration and had big porches encircling their fronts. Now the paint was peeling and faded and the front yards were overgrown with weeds. Toni stopped outside a house that looked even more faded than the others. A shutter hung from one hinge, flapping idly in the breeze, and the concrete front path was badly cracked. A sign taped to the front door read Apartments for Rent. See Owner R. Paolini, Second Floor.

When Toni looked at the house, her eye didn't linger on the peeling paint or the overgrown front yard. Instead she was riveted by the dormer windows of the attic rooms. They looked so cozy and inviting, peeping out from under the gingerbread trim of the roof. She bounded up the front steps and pushed at the front door. It swung open, and she found herself in a dark hallway. Inside there was a faint fishy smell, and the dark wood reminded her a lot of Jill's college dorm at Rosemont. *Funny that we're both going to be living in the same sort of place*, she thought.

Her footsteps sounded unnaturally loud as she walked across the hall to get to the stairs. A door on her right opened as she passed, and an old woman's face, framed by wispy white hair, poked out. "Peekaboo!" she said.

Toni looked back. "Peekaboo," she answered uneasily.

"No, not you!" the old woman snapped.

Toni looked around, but the hallway was deserted.

"Sorry," she muttered, and started to climb the stairs. *I wonder if that's why they always have vacancies here*, she thought. *The house is probably full of loonies.*

She heard the old woman calling out, "Peekaboo. Peekaboo . . ." as she entered the darkness of the upstairs hallway. A sign on the first door said clearly R. Paolini. Owner, Manager.

Toni tapped nervously. She waited what seemed like a long while, then tapped again. The door was opened so quickly and violently that she almost toppled backward down the stairs.

"Yes! What-a you want?" a man roared at her in a foreign-accented voice.

Toni took in the round flabby face, the unruly gray hair, the T-shirt that didn't quite stretch over a flabby stomach.

50

"I've . . . er . . . come about an apartment," she stammered.

"What about it?" he roared again.

"I want to rent one. Do you have any free?"

He looked at her as if he were deciding whether she would be likely to bring in all of the Hell's Angels complete with their motorcycles.

"How many people?" he asked at last.

"Just me."

"That's what they all say," he growled. "They say just-a one person, then they bring all-a their friends to live here, too."

"I say just one person and mean just one person," Toni reiterated, beginning to feel angry. "Do you have a vacancy or not?"

The man nodded slowly. "Sure. I have-a room free. Upstairs. Might not-a be what you want."

"May I see it, please?" Toni asked politely.

He grunted, scowling at her. Then he led the way up another flight of stairs to an even smaller hallway above. "It's-a okay for just one person," he said. "You have steady work to pay for this?"

"I'm a secretary," Tony replied frostily.

"Hmmmph," he said, as if he thought she was probably, in reality, a pickpocket or a stripper. He flung open the door. "Here it is," he said. "Kitchen facilities, but bathroom down-a the hall."

The first thing Toni saw when she stepped inside was the view through the window. Between the buildings opposite she could just glimpse Puget

Sound glistening in the distance and the mountains looming beyond. That view convinced her instantly that this was the right place for her.

"I'll take it," she said, giving a quick glance around the room, noting the curtain in the corner that when closed, would hide the little sink, the stove, and the small refrigerator now visible; the bright flower-covered sofa bed; the rickety table and two chairs; and the brilliant yellow chest of drawers.

"Don't you want-a to see the bathroom?" he asked, astonished.

"I'm sure it's fine," Toni said happily. All she knew was that she had a mountain view from her window and that the room was full of bright, happy colors. "When can I move in?"

"Soon as you pay me a month's rent," Mr. Paolini said, "plus a cleaning deposit."

"How about tomorrow?" Toni said excitedly.

"Fine." He shrugged his shoulders. "But remember, I don't want no trouble here. Understand me? No wild parties and lots of noise. I got enough of that from the kids next door. This-a place is full of quiet, ordinary people. I want to keep it that way."

"Don't worry," Toni said. "I'll be very quiet."

He nodded, then he stood staring, as if he were watching something.

After a while Toni became uneasy. "Is something wrong, Mr. Paolini?" she asked.

"They're all around us-a, you know," he said in a low voice. "Don't you feel them?"

"No—what?" Toni asked in alarm, wondering if he was talking about fleas or spies.

"Spirits," Mr. Paolini said reverently. "The spirit world is-a all around us. I feel it. And I'm one of the few people they will talk to. . . . I'll see you tomorrow then, Miss."

With that he turned and walked down the stairs, leaving a slightly scared and puzzled Toni standing in the middle of her new room.

As she turned to make her way down the stairs the door opposite opened and two young men in jeans and slickers came out. Immediately Toni was overpowered by a strong smell of fish. The two men grinned when they saw her. "You moving in here?" one of them asked pleasantly.

Toni nodded.

They both smiled. "Terrific," the taller one said. "You're a big improvement on the last tenant—she used to sing hymns in the bathtub."

"And take hours," the other added. "There's only one bathroom to a floor so the matter was often rather urgent. Do you work around here?"

"I'm a student and I'm working in an office, too," Toni said.

"Busy girl," the taller, sandy-haired one said, smiling at her. "I bet you can't guess what we do?"

"It's rather obvious that we work on a fishing boat," the other cut in. "But it's just our work clothes that smell like this. You should see us when we're ready to check out the discos. I'm Dan, by the way, and this is Chris."

"My name is Toni," she said, smiling with relief at the open, friendly faces. "And I'm glad to meet you. I was beginning to think everyone here was a little, you know—"

Dan and Chris laughed. "Uh-oh. It sounds like Mr. Paolini told you about his spirit friends."

"Ye-es," Toni said hesitantly. "This house isn't really haunted, is it?"

Dan laughed. "If it is, then nobody's seen the spirits except Mr. Paolini. He talks to them all the time, but don't let that worry you . . ."

"And what about the old woman on the first floor who said 'Peekaboo' to me, then got angry when I answered her?"

The boys threw back their heads and laughed. "She wasn't talking to you," Tony said. "She was calling her dog. She has this little Pekingese and she calls it Peekaboo! Very confusing . . . It's always wandering off and she's always calling it."

Toni started to laugh. "Oh, well. At least this doesn't sound like a boring place to live. I think I'm going to like it here," she said.

SIX

"Jill?"

"Toni—is that you?" Jill answered.

"Who else would take the trouble to call you at seven-thirty in the morning?" came back Toni's amused voice. "I'll bet you're still in your robe, half-asleep."

"I'm awake now. Is something wrong, Toni?"

"Nothing—why should something be wrong?"

"I just got a letter from you yesterday."

"Well, I decided to call you today and invite you to dinner when you come home this weekend."

"That's why you called? Toni, you're an idiot! You know I'd love to have dinner with you when I come home."

"But I thought you might not know the address."

"Strangely enough, my brain hasn't been to-tally drained during two months of college. I can still remember that I go down the hill, turn right, make a left on Birch Avenue, and there I am."

"Wrong!"

"Oooh! Don't say that word—you sound like my English professor. Anyway, what do you mean, 'wrong'? Has your family moved or something?"

"No, they're right where they were . . ."

"Then has somebody moved my house to another block without telling me?"

Toni giggled. She'd been trying to play this phone call very coolly but the giggle had been bubbling up irresistibly the whole time. "Nobody moved except me, Jill. I phoned to tell you that I now have my own apartment."

"Toni—no kidding—your own apartment?"

"That's right. I am now a mature adult, surviving on my own."

"Who are you sharing it with?"

"Nobody. I have my own studio."

"Toni! How can you afford that?"

"Oh, I'm making good money at my job, you know."

"But that's fantastic. I'm very impressed. Tell me all about it."

"Well, it's on the top floor, a sort of penthouse with a fabulous view . . . right across Puget Sound, and very bright Danish sort of furniture, and a dear little kitchen . . ."

"It sounds wonderful. But how on earth did you find something like that?"

"Just sheer genius, I suppose . . ."

"Toni, you are impossible. I can't wait to see you."

"And wait until you see the meal I'm serving—none of that pallid college fare. This will be pure gourmet."

"But you don't know how to boil an egg, Toni."

"Correction—I *didn't* know how to boil an egg. Now I am very into haute cuisine. Rosemont College isn't the only place where you learn fancy new skills, you know."

"Toni—I'm very impressed. You make me feel like a little schoolkid. Here you are doing all these grown-up things—a real job, a real apartment, cooking for yourself, while I still have to sign in with the housemother at night and obey a bunch of stupid rules."

"Well, yeah, I guess my dad's heart attack changed a lot of things for me," Toni said. "But it's really terrific to be my own boss, Jill. I love it. There are some kids from college in the house next door and they have nonstop parties. . . . And there are these two supercute fishermen on my floor. I'm only a few minutes away from college, so I don't even have to get up until eight-thirty . . ."

"But, Toni, what do your folks think about this?"

"They're not exactly thrilled. In fact, we had a big fight about it before I left. My dad's really upset. Ever since his heart attack, he's become so super-protective. Now he's convinced there'll be muggers forcing their way into my apartment, explosions because I left the stove on by mistake, and my early death by malnutrition because I'm not eating right. You name it, he's worried about it, Jill. . . . But it was really for his sake that I moved out. I kept thinking that, maybe, if I got out of the way, he'd have to start living again and getting up and doing things. He's really recovered nicely, except for this mental block he has. I'm just sure that the moment he decides he's not an invalid, he'll be fine. I plan to ask him to help me put up shelves and stuff in a while. Maybe that will get his interest back."

"It must've been a hard decision for you to make . . . to move out and leave him right now."

"I've been going over and over it in my mind. I kept on thinking—what if worrying about me causes another heart attack? How would I feel then? But I decided he'd worry about me more if I was around all the time. Do you know, he wanted to know what bus I was coming home on every day and exactly what time it was supposed to arrive? I couldn't live like that, Jill. I'd have gone bananas really quickly, or worse still, I'd have lost my temper and said all sorts of horrible things I didn't really mean. So it was for me, too, that I decided to get out. I've got to get on with my own life . . ."

"Of course you do, and I think you made a wise choice. I bet your dad will be very proud of the way you're handling things on your own."

"I hope so. In fact, the dinner for you will be a trial run. If that goes well, then I'll invite my parents to a meal."

"Oh, so I'm the guinea pig, huh? If I don't die of food poisoning, you'll invite them? Thanks a lot."

"You will not die of food poisoning. You might faint with bliss at the wonderful flavors and delicate aromas . . ."

"When would you like me to show up for this blissful dinner?"

"Saturday, at seven, can you make it?"

"Sure, give me the address. And consider yourself very honored, because I'm seeing you even before I see Craig!"

"Wow—am I ever honored. I thought you'd run right into his arms the moment you got back."

"I would if his arms were around to run into. . . . I got a postcard with two lines scribbled on it saying that he's got an away football game on Saturday so he won't be able to see me until Sunday . . ."

"He plays football now? I can't believe that!"

Jill giggled. "No, he's joined the marching band."

"Phew. That sounds more like Craig. I couldn't imagine him getting stomped on and all covered with mud!"

"I hardly know what to imagine about him, anymore, Toni. He seems to be so busy all the time. I mean, he never seems to have much time for me. I suppose I'm being too sensitive, but I get worried that—"

"—that what? He'll find somebody else?"

"No, not so much that. Just that he may realize he can survive perfectly well without me. . . . Listen, let's stop all this dumb talk. I'm sure everything will be fine this weekend. Look, I'll be at your 'penthouse' on the dot of seven Saturday! I can hardly wait, Toni!"

"Me either, Jill!"

The big bell in the college clock tower chimed seven as Jill knocked on Toni's front door.

"Good timing," Toni said, opening the door to reveal herself wearing an apron saying BON APPÉTIT. "We gourmet cooks get very temperamental if our guests don't show up on time."

"Toni, you look great," Jill said, "but don't expect me to hug you until you have washed all that sticky goop off your hands."

Toni swept ahead of Jill into the room. "Great chefs always get sticky hands," she said. "Look at Julia Child—she always plunges up to her elbows in her dough. Did you find the place okay?"

"No problem, except I had some weird encounters coming up the stairs. First this old woman put her head out the door and said 'Peekaboo' to me and then an old man came out into the hall and said he'd just been speaking to his mother! He can't have a mother who's still alive, can he?"

Toni grinned. "Oh, no, she's been dead for about fifteen years," she said calmly. "It's her spirit he talks to . . . and everyone else's spirit too."

The Trouble with Toni

"Toni—how horrible! Aren't you scared to be in the same house with those crazies?"

Toni shrugged her shoulders. "Oh, they're not that crazy. Mrs. Crowe on the ground floor was only calling her Pekingese dog, and if you ignore the fact that he speaks to spirits, Mr. Paolini is perfectly normal."

Jill gazed around the room, taking everything in for the first time. She looked at the peeling roses on the walls, the big hole in the carpet, the table propped up on a telephone book, the bright pinks and oranges of the sofa cover, which clashed with the red of the wallpaper and the yellow of the chest, and the line of Toni's laundry drying on the curtain rod that separated kitchen from living space. Then she looked at Toni's glowing face . . .

"It's great, Toni," she said. "It's everything you need."

"It is, isn't it?" Toni said. "I mean, who needs a closet, anyway? Most of my clothes are jeans, and I can just shove them in those drawers over there. And when I can find a poster that doesn't clash with the wallpaper, I'll put that up, too. But the view is great, isn't it?"

Jill looked out the window at the dark brick office buildings and the elevated expressway snaking beyond them. Between them a tiny patch of water and a glimpse of distant hills were visible.

"It's a wonderful view, Toni," she said.

"I knew you'd like it," Toni said happily. "My mother didn't, I could tell. When she helped me move my stuff, she said she wasn't sure about leaving her only daughter in such a fleabag. But I like it."

"Well, that's the only thing that matters," Jill said. "You know how middle-aged people get about comfort. They want everything to look as if it came out of a Sears catalog, but you and I don't. Now how about that dinner—I'm starving."

"Please be seated, Madame—no, not that chair. One of the legs doesn't work! Now, I had planned to start with the crab cocktail . . ."

"Toni—how extravagant!"

"But I didn't quite manage to get it ready. I thought you might just help me with the last stages of preparation. I couldn't do it all myself."

"Sure, I'll help. What do you want me to do, cut up stuff?"

"Not exactly. Take a look in here, okay?" She walked into the kitchen and came out with a bucket. Jill peeped in curiously, then screamed.

"Toni, there are live crabs in there! You want to make a crab cocktail out of live crabs?"

"They were supposed to be dead by the time they got into the cocktail."

"But are you out of your mind? What made you buy live crabs? You can go to any supermarket and get crabmeat—all out of the shell and wrapped in plastic."

"Well, it wasn't really my idea," Toni said, looking at the scrabbling legs in the bucket. "You see, I told the two fishermen next door that I was preparing a fancy dinner, and they left these outside my door as a gift. I knocked on their door to see if they were still home and if they'd kill the crabs for me, but they were gone. They go out at night in their boat a lot."

"So what are we going to do?" Jill asked hesitantly.

"I thought you might kill them for me."

"What made you think that? Do you remember how I was after my one fishing trip? I couldn't even put the bait on the hook without getting nauseated."

"But what about me? I feel sick to my stomach if I squash a spider. Come on, Jill. It's not hard. You just put them in warm water and gradually heat it up. They're not supposed to feel a thing."

"How do you know? Have you ever been a crab? And what if they do feel something? What if they start screaming in agony or climbing out over the side of the pot?"

"Oh, shut up, please. Let's just admit it. We're both too chicken to boil them."

"Right."

The two girls stood there looking down at the waving claws.

"What am I going to do with them, Jill?"

"Keep them as pets?"

"Very funny. Can you imagine lying there in the dark at night, hearing all those little legs skittering across the floor and wondering if they were about to climb into bed with you?"

"Then keep them in the bathtub!" Jill said, starting to laugh.

Toni began to laugh, too. "Slight problem. My bathroom is shared by five other people. If old Mrs. Hansen went in to take her morning bath . . ."

"Oh, Toni," Jill said at last, "why do such crazy things always happen to you? We'll take the creepy-crawly things down to the water in the morning and release them."

"Actually," Toni said, peering into the bucket, "when you look at them closely, they are sort of cute. Look at their beady little eyes swiveling around. I wish my eyes were on stalks, then I could cheat on math tests and nobody would know. Okay, we'll take them back in the morning. But in the meantime, we have no appetizer. Do you mind starting with the main course?"

"That will be fine with me," Jill said. "I'm getting pretty hungry. I hope there's a lot."

"I think I cooked enough," Toni said. "But I wasn't too sure about how much to put in." She pulled the curtain aside and went through into the kitchen. "It should be . . . ahhh!"

"What is it, Toni?"

"Don't come in . . ."

"But, Toni?"

"I said don't come in."

Jill dashed through the curtain, knocking down some of Toni's laundry. "What on earth is that?" she said, staring at the large pot on the stove top. Originally it had been covered by a lid, but the lid was now pushed up in the air by a huge mound of bright red, slimy stuff, oozing over the top and beginning to drip onto the floor.

"It's dinner," Toni said in a subdued voice.

"It looks more like the Incredible Blob! What is it supposed to be?"

"Spaghetti," Toni said. "Italian food is very in right now."

"I've never seen spaghetti that looked like that before," Jill said, still staring at the stove in horror. "It's bright red."

"That's because I've only got one pot," Toni said. "This place wasn't as fully furnished as they claimed. So I decided to cook the spaghetti and the sauce at the same time. After all, you mix them together when you're done, don't you?"

"But why is it climbing out of the pot? It wasn't alive like the crabs to start with, was it?"

Toni's face, which had been tense with disappointment, twitched into a smile. "Maybe I put in a little too much spaghetti?" she asked.

"How much did you put it?"

"Two boxes."

"Two boxes?" Jill shrieked.

"Well, one box didn't look like enough, and I knew we were both going to be hungry."

"Toni, two boxes is enough to feed twenty people."

"Well, how was I supposed to know the spaghetti was going to grow the minute I turned my back? It just looked like a few skinny dry sticks when I dropped it in. Maybe it tastes all right. Do you want to try some?"

"I don't know," Jill said hesitantly. "It looks too much like the scene of a mass murder."

"Thanks a lot," Toni said. "Now you've made me lose my appetite, too. I guess we better go right to the dessert. I know there can't be anything wrong with that, because it came from a mix and all I had to do was follow the directions."

"Thank goodness for that," Jill muttered.

Toni opened the oven and peered in. "That's funny," she said.

"What's funny?" Jill asked in a sinking voice.

"It said on the box only to cook for twenty-five minutes. This has had more than half an hour, but it doesn't look done yet." She pulled out a tray of slopping brown liquid.

"What is it?" Jill asked doubtfully.

"Brownies."

"Brownies? Brownies don't look like that, Toni. I've made brownies hundreds of times. They never look like that, even at the beginning. You must have done something wrong."

"How could I have done something wrong?" Toni snapped. "I followed all the directions!"

Jill rummaged through the garbage and brought out the empty brownie-mix box. "Did you add one egg?" she asked.

"Of course I did. And I did everything else right, too. I can read, you know."

"And three tablespoons of water?"

"Three tablespoons?" Toni's voice trembled. "I thought it said three cups."

"Three cups?" Jill squeaked. "Toni—you only use three cups of water when you're making orange juice!"

"Oh," Toni said. "I guess I blew that one, too." She turned away from Jill and walked over to the window. "I wanted so much to make a dinner all by myself," she said. "But nowadays it seems as though I blow everything. Sometimes I think I can't do anything right."

Jill walked over and put her hand on her friend's shoulder. "There's lots of things you can do, Toni. It's just that you were brought up in a family where both of your parents worked—so nobody ever cooked anything. How could you possibly expect to learn to put a meal together overnight? I've been helping my mom make brownies since I was a little kid, because that's the way it was in our house—she stayed home and cooked. All you ever did was open cans and thaw frozen dinners while your mom was down in her studio hacking away at some sculpture. You just need a little practice and you'll be fine."

Toni shook her head and didn't look at Jill. "I really began to hope that things were getting better," she said in a choked voice.

"What do you mean, better?" Jill asked. "Everything's going so well for you. You're taking all those practical courses at college—I know I could never learn computer programming—you've got this dream job in theater, and now you've got your own apartment. What more could you want?"

"Nothing, I guess," Toni said evenly. "I suppose I must be very happy." She stood there, playing with the tassel at the edge of the curtain, swishing it back and forth.

"Toni?" Jill said gently at last. "Would you like to come out for pizza with me? Maybe then we could talk about everything."

SEVEN

"It's all been like a bad dream," Toni said, delicately picking an olive from the top of her slice of pizza and popping it into her mouth. That in itself would have been enough to convince Jill that all was not well with Toni. Toni was famous for devouring an entire pizza, single-handedly, in thirty seconds. "First there was my father's heart attack, and then I had to watch you go off to college without me . . . I'm a good actress, Jill. Everyone kept saying, 'Oh, Toni's so strong. She's holding up so well.' and I kept on saying to myself, 'Yeah, you'd better get it all together because everyone expects you to.' So I just kept on smiling and saying that everything was fine."

"But everything is fine now, isn't it?" Jill asked, sounding concerned. "I know that community college isn't the same as the university, but you're doing so well there. . . . And the job and the apartment—you sounded so excited on the phone!"

"I kept telling myself everything was about to get better," Toni said pulling at a strand of cheese so that it stretched to an enormous length before popping loose, "but now I'm not sure. You see, now I'm beginning to wonder if I belong anywhere—and that's a scary feeling, Jill."

"Uuum—I know," Jill said. "But you'll get over it, I'm sure. I felt just the same way when I started at Rosemont. I looked around at all those kids who seemed so sure of themselves—and I asked myself, 'What am I doing here? Everyone else is so smart and so rich and maybe I don't belong here.' Then I found out that a lot of the people I met were all thinking the same thing. I bet that's what's happening to you. Maybe all the other students in your classes are just waiting to make friends, too . . ."

"Oh, sure, if I want to join the Golden Oldies club," Toni said. "Half of my classes are filled with these middle-aged executive type women. And, Jill, the others—the airheads from high school—the only goal in life any of them has is to be a secretary until some rich guy sweeps her off her feet and asks her to marry him. They even look like secretaries already, memorizing their steno and stuff. I'm the only dummy in the whole business math class. We had to do a pretend budget reconciliation—you know, that's when you tie in all the invoices with what you've got on paper—and I was three million dollars off in my calculations. Three million dollars, Jill! I don't think any real company would hire someone who kept the books that way. The teacher told me that getting thirty cents wrong is considered a big mistake!"

Jill tried to keep a straight face, but her mouth twitched into a smile. "Don't laugh, it's not funny," Toni said hopelessly.

"It is, really, Toni," Jill said. "Go on, finish your slice of pizza. You'll feel better with some food in your stomach."

"Yes, I admit, it is nice to have some real food for a change," Toni said, taking an experimental bite of pizza.

"Do you mean you're not eating right, now that you're on your own?"

"It depends on what you mean by eating right," Toni said cautiously. "I'm very good with cans, but there doesn't happen to be a can opener in my apartment. I'm planning on making a midnight raid on my parents and carrying off all the things my apartment doesn't have. An electric heater, to begin with! The building is supposed to be heated, but the theory that hot air rises doesn't work as far as my room is concerned. The air rises to the floor below me and then comes down again. My room is freezing at night already! By the time winter really comes I'll have to chip the ice off my blankets before I get up! There are so many things I need, Jill, and I don't ever have time to go shopping. I get up, rush to classes, rush from classes to my job, and then come home to study. Some days I feel like I'm running up a down escalator and however fast I try

71

to move forward, I stay in the same place or start slipping backward again."

Jill looked into her friend's troubled face. "I wish I knew what to say, Toni," she said. "Maybe you're trying to do too much and you should slow down for a while . . ."

"But how can I?" Toni snapped. "If I don't make some money, I'll never be able to escape from community college, and there's no way I'm moving back home right now. My nerves were ready to snap there. No, I've got to keep on going, Jill, even if I do hate it all."

"But there must be some good parts to your day. You said the computer instructor was cute?"

"Toni sighed. "He is. He also speaks a language I don't speak. When I ask him for help he explains very patiently, but it's like someone talking to me in Chinese. I keep wanting to blurt out to him, 'I don't even understand the basic things.' There's no point in his telling me how to call a file into the memory, because I don't understand what the memory is. I guess my brain wasn't made to understand computers."

"Maybe you're taking the wrong courses, then," Jill said. "It sound like you're trying to train yourself to be the kind of person other people want you to be. That can put too much stress on someone, Toni. I think you should take another look at the catalog and say to yourself, 'What would I really love to do?' I'm surprised you aren't taking any theater courses—that's what you love most, isn't it?"

"Sure," Toni said, "but who knows if I have enough talent to make it in the theater? Besides, right now I have to concentrate on practical things . . ."

"Not if they're making you nervous and depressed and you can't do them, anyway," Jill said. "But there's always your job. You're enjoying that, aren't you?"

"I guess so," Toni said, and went back to picking olives from the remainder of the pizza.

"So it's not as good as you thought it was going to be?" Jill asked.

Toni shrugged her shoulders. "I just figured . . . it doesn't matter. It's dumb, anyway."

"It does matter, Toni. You can tell me. That's what best friends are for! What did you think it would be like?"

"That it would be more like a theater job. But it's just an office job that happens to be in a theater building. I had this daydream about taking notes from the producer and ordering costumes and all that sort of stuff. Instead all I do is typing and filing and mailing. I send out subscription reminders. I take ticket orders over the phone. That's about it. The job wouldn't be bad, I guess, if—if there were other people. . . . That's the real problem, Jill. I'm lonely. Suddenly I don't have anybody I can talk to. I go to classes every day and I say a few polite words to people. I come home and I say a few polite words . . ."

"What about the kids next door with the wild parties?" Jill interrupted.

"I went to one," Toni said. "That is not my scene, Jill. Their idea of fun is booze and drugs. I could never be like that."

"Of course not," Jill agreed. "But you told me you liked the people you work with?"

"Oh, I do," Toni said. "They're really nice to me. But it's almost as if I'm their pet robot or something. They live in such a different world. Both Judy and Pam have little kids, and their entire conversation is about diaper rashes and the Terrible Twos. I get scared when I look at them. They're not much older than I am, but they're already in such a rut. And Mrs. Thompson is nice, but I always feel like I'm on my best behavior with her. I have the feeling she's watching me, as if she's waiting for me to screw up so she can say, 'See, you aren't skilled enough for this job. You blew it.'"

"Oh, I'm sure that's not true," Jill said.

Toni smiled. "Maybe not. Maybe I'm just getting paranoid. Maybe next I'll start talking to spirits . . ."

Jill laughed. "Toni Redmond—all you need right now is some real food, and enough rest, and courses at college that really interest you. As soon as you start doing things you like, you'll meet people you like. Look at me and the newspaper. Now I know lots of people, just through that. Isn't there a school play coming up you could try out for?"

"They've already cast the fall play," Toni said. "But I think you may be right. I should sign up for some drama classes next quarter. At least it would convince the people at work that I know a little bit about the theater. They all treat me as if I'm a total newcomer. They say things like, 'That's stage talk for . . .' and they talk about their actors and actresses as if they were only one notch below God. When that leading lady actually deigned to speak to me I almost thought they wanted to kiss my hand!"

"Some day that will be you," Jill said.

"I wish."

"I know you can do it, Toni. Just go for it!"

"Well . . . I don't know . . ."

"Come on, you can do it," Jill urged.

Toni's face broke into a grin. "Okay," she said.

"That's more like the old Toni," Jill said. "I can just see those women at your office when you get to be a big star some day and come back . . ."

"Yeah, and they'll fight over who's going to sit next to me and who's going to make me coffee," Toni said, her eyes shining. "Hey, you know what? I feel a lot better. No more disasters for me. From now on, my cooking will be limited to frozen dinners. What do you say we go have a huge sundae over at Eduardo's across the street—my treat?"

"Great idea," Jill said, getting up. "I knew there was no way to keep you down for long, Toni Redmond. You're unsinkable."

"Only because you help me keep my head above water," Toni said. "I think I'll kidnap you and keep you locked in my room. I'm scared that when you go back, I'll start panicking again!"

"Panic is strictly forbidden," Jill said firmly. "I've just looked into my crystal ball and I hereby predict that everything is about to get better and better for you. Good things are right around the corner, Toni—I know it!"

"I hope so," Toni said. "Oh, I really hope so!"

EIGHT

During the next week Toni wondered more than once whether Jill really did have magic powers. Jill had predicted that things were going to change for Toni, and they did change—although maybe not in the way Jill had in mind.

On Monday morning Toni gave herself a pep talk as she left her apartment. "No more feeling sorry for yourself, Redmond!" she said severely as she ran, late as usual, down the block. "Everything's going to be just fine. You're going to make friends, get into fun classes, do so well at your job that you become the key person in the theater, the one everyone comes to for advice . . ." She let herself daydream as she rushed along. She imagined herself sitting at her desk, typing with flying fingers, a telephone cradled at each ear while she fired off answers to questions from all sides: The programs? Yes, I've designed them myself and they're already at the printer. Yes, I'd be delighted to come and help with casting. No, that color is quite wrong for the leading lady's dress in Act Two. Try purple. How about November third for the big fund-raiser? I've already extended a personal invitation to the mayor . . .

A horn honked as she almost stepped in the path of a car. She came back to earth with a thud and stood, grinning, at the curb. "Back to the real world, Redmond," she admonished herself.

The morning at college was uneventful. Each of her classes seemed more monotonous than the one before. But when she arrived at work, out of breath from running, she found that lots of exciting things had been happening there.

". . . And he just started yelling at her," Pam was saying as Toni reached the doorway. "He told her if she couldn't take the trouble to learn her lines, then she'd better get out right now."

"Wow," Judy said. "Did she get mad? She's not exactly the type of person you yell at!"

"She just smiled sweetly and said, 'But, darling, it's two whole weeks to the opening night. I'll be fine by then!' Then Brandt really blew his top and said he was sick of working with amateurs and if he had his way he'd throw her out on the spot! Then she just smiled and said, 'But, darling, if I leave, there won't be any play!' Then everyone started yelling and Brandt called off the rehearsal."

"Who was this?" Toni asked from the doorway. They looked up, noticing her for the first time. "Adriana," Judy said, as if they weren't too anxious to discuss the flap with Toni. "They had a fight at rehearsal this weekend."

"She's the mermaid, right?" Toni asked. "The blond lady who came in here once?"

"Right," Pam said.

"So did she get thrown out?" Toni wanted to know.

"I hope not," Pam said. "Because if she goes, we don't have a mermaid. And if we don't have a mermaid, we don't have a show."

"That would be terrible," Judy agreed. "Everything would fall apart. Brandt really shouldn't lose his temper. Maybe he's not right for an amateur group like this. . . . After all, you can't afford to offend people like Adriana!"

"He's too young," Pam said, going back to her desk. "You need someone mature for his job. I'm surprised they gave it to him. Serve the committee right if the whole play falls apart . . ."

"Do you think that might happen?" Toni asked, looking at the huge pile of announcements on her desk. "Because I don't want to send out thousands of flyers for a play that isn't going to be performed."

"Just keep sending out announcements," Pam said firmly, "and forget about what you heard just now."

Toni sat at her desk and starting typing labels. She was fuming. What right did Pam and Judy have to snap at her like that? All day she felt just like Cinderella, being picked on by two ugly stepsisters.

Around six Mrs. Thompson herself swept into the office—two frown lines creasing the makeup on her normally flawless face.

"Oh, Toni," she said, glancing across at Toni's desk. "Aren't those announcements out yet?"

Toni opened her mouth to say, "They were only delivered from the printer on Friday, remember?" but before she could say a thing Mrs. Thompson went on. "I thought I made it clear to you how important it was that they be sent out last week! You're going to have to show more responsibility if you want to stay with us. After all, there is no point in putting on a play if we have no audience to see it, is there?" Her mouth twitched into a smile that didn't quite reach her eyes.

"From what I heard there might not be a play," Toni said, before she could stop herself. She realized immediately that she had made a mistake. The smile vanished from Mrs. Thompson's face altogether. "I do not want to hear that sort of gossip repeated again," she said icily. "Do you have any idea of the harm that bad publicity can do to us? Just because there was a little misunderstanding over the weekend . . . That has all been smoothed over. Actors are artists, after all . . . such temperamental people. Anyway, not another word about it, even around the office. You never know who might be listening . . ."

Toni thought it was hardly likely that a spy could have made his way up three floors just to overhear gossip about an amateur theater. But she kept her thoughts to herself and muttered, "No, Mrs. Thompson."

That made Mrs. Thompson attempt a smile again. "Good girl," she said. "And remember— responsibility, Toni. Don't let us down. You will stay on to finish those tonight, won't you? And make sure that everything is locked up when you leave. We have so many valuable props down in the theater now, antiques that are on loan to us."

It was more a command than a request, so Toni stayed. The others left together around six-thirty. Toni heard the sound of their voices fading, then the elevator creaking and groaning as it disappeared downward. She tried to get through the announcements as quickly as possible, but the light in the office was poor, her brain was tired, and she kept making mistakes. She was very conscious of being all alone in an old building in a not-too-desirable part of town. She remembered how she had told Mrs. Thompson that she was quite happy about working late hours. Now she didn't feel at all happy. The old building seemed full of noises, the creaking of wood and the thumping of water pipes, the drip of a faucet in the bathroom. Each sound made Toni jump. She realized that if anybody broke in and came up in the elevator, she would be hopelessly trapped, with nobody for miles around to hear her scream. She walked over to the window and peered down into the alleyway below. One lone steet lamp cast a small pool of light in the surrounding darkness. Toni did not look forward to stepping out into that alleyway . . .

She made herself a cup of instant coffee, then sat down and started typing furiously again. No matter how many labels she typed and stuck on the flyers, the pile of announcements never seemed to get any smaller. *I'm so tired,* she thought, resting her head in her arms on the desktop. Her eyes closed. She must have drifted off to sleep because she woke with a start, her heart thumping.

Something had waked her. She sat, tense and listening, waiting for the noise to be repeated. For a long while she sat there, holding her breath, the only sound the blood pounding in her head, then she heard it again—a scraping, dragging noise, coming from beneath the floorboards. She knelt down and put her ear to the floor. No voices, just the sound of something heavy being dragged. She remembered what Mrs. Thompson had said: "Valuable antiques . . . On loan to us . . . Responsibility, Toni!"

With trembling fingers Toni picked up the phone and dialed. "Hello, police," she whispered. "Somebody has broken into the Theater Alliance building and I'm trapped upstairs. I think they're stealing furniture. Please hurry."

There was no lock on the office door. Toni listened for the sound of the elevator, wondering what she would do if she heard it coming up. Then, when she thought she couldn't bear to be alone for another minute, she heard a car drive up. From her window she could see the flashing red light. She hurried down the hall to press the elevator button, then ran back to the office. Snatching up her coat and handbag, she waited, keeping the office door open a crack to see if anyone got off the elevator when it arrived. No one did. Walking softly she retraced her steps and peeked into the open elevator. Empty! She jumped in and waited impatiently as it descended to the ground floor.

"Thank heavens you came," she panted, rushing over to the two policemen who had entered the alleyway. "I was scared they would come upstairs next."

"Where did you year the noise, miss?" one policeman asked kindly.

"Down in the theater. It sounded like someone dragging something heavy."

"You wait out here," he said. "We'll go take a look." Toni followed at a safe distance as they walked around to the front of the theater. She heard one policeman say to the other, "She's right. The door isn't properly closed all the way. Let's go take a look . . ."

They disappeared into the building. Toni waited, shivering, beside the police car. Suppose they caught a burglar, all because of her! "He was just about to make off with the antique sofa," Mrs.

Thompson would say. "But our responsible Toni called the police just in time. She deserves a medal!"

Suddenly the doors burst open, and the policemen came out again, dragging between them a tall young man, dressed in shabby cords and a frayed gray sweater. He was struggling, but they had a good hold on him.

"Will you let go of me," he yelled. For an instant Toni was sorry she'd called the police, because the young man was very good-looking—with a wild, haunted look to his face. Lots of terrible, improbable thoughts began to go through Toni's head: he had been out of a job for months, his wife and baby were starving, and finally in desperation he was searching the theater to see if any food had been left around. She was about to beg the policemen to be gentle with him and to hear his side of the story, when they dragged him over to her.

"All right, miss. Do you know this man?" they asked.

She was torn. Should she try to save him from a life in jail? "No, I don't," she finally came clean. "I've never seen him before."

"See, I told you, Jake," one policeman said to the other. "He's a smooth talker."

"I've never seen her before, either," the young man said, his eyes blazing as he eyed Toni. "Did it occur to you that *she* might have broken in?"

"I didn't break in. I work here," Toni said frostily.

"Then how come I've never seen you?" the young man demanded.

"I only started last week," she said.

The young man turned to his police escort. "That should explain everything, officers. She only started here last week. If she'd been around any longer, she would be able to tell you that I happen to be the director of this play."

Toni stared at him, openmouthed. "You're Brandt?" she asked.

"I'm Brandt," he said coldly. "Brandt Caldwell. If you'd care to call Mrs. Thompson I'm sure she'd be happy to identify me."

"If you're the director, how come you sneaked in without turning on any lights?" the policeman Jake asked, "and why were you dragging away that sofa?"

"I can explain that," the young man said. "We need to have the sofa recovered for the play. I managed to borrow a friend's truck tonight so I drove by to get the sofa. I don't need the big lights on. I know my way around the theater blindfolded."

One of the policemen finished looking through Brandt's papers. He handed them back. "Here you are, sir. We seem to have made a mistake. But the young lady was absolutely right to call us when she heard suspicious noises late at night."

Brandt looked at Toni coldly. "There are often suspicious noises in theaters late at night," he said.

"She'd better get used to that if she wants to go on working here."

"I'm sorry," Toni said. "But you wouldn't have been too happy if you'd come back in the morning and found your set cleaned out, would you?"

"I guess not," Brandt admitted, his tone softening. "But next time, if you hear strange noises, call down first on the house phone. If a burglar answers, *then* call the police, okay?" He brushed himself off and walked back toward the theater. "Now, if you gentlemen will excuse me, I have a sofa to move out."

"We'll give you a hand, sir," one of the policemen said. "Hold the door open, Jake."

The three men disappeared into the building, leaving Toni on the sidewalk. She hung around for a few moments, not sure if she should wait and apologize or disappear quietly. *The one cute guy I've met in so long, and I blew it, she thought. . . . If only I'd known a hunk like that was working downstairs . . . I could have offered to make him some coffee, help carry his sofas around . . . but it's too late now. The way he looked at me, something tells me the sooner I disappear, the better.*

NINE

Toni was so mad at herself for her stupid mistake that, for the next few days, she tried to be a model person Friday. She worked extra hard. She offered to make coffee. She ran and mailed things and she even got the printer to reduce the bill because he had delivered the announcements two days late. Then one day she had to stay late in computer science to finish a spread sheet. She just missed one bus and the next one seemed to crawl along. When the bus finally stopped at the water-front, Toni leaped off and rushed across the street. Mrs. Thompson had made a little remark the day before about responsible people showing up on time. Mrs. Thompson, Toni was discovering, was very good at making little remarks. She never actually came right out and criticized, but you ended up feeling much worse after her not-so-gentle hints. Her favorite hint at the moment was that Toni was still only in a trial period and could be thrown out if she didn't shape up. Toni had the feeling that showing up an hour late might fall into the category of not shaping up.

She bounded up the iron steps, two at a time, wrenched open the glass door, saw the elevator door just closing, and flung herself inside.

"Don't press that—" a voice yelled in her ear as her finger came in contact with the Up button. "—button," the voice finished just as she pressed the little black knob. She turned in horror to find herself staring straight at Brandt. He was not dressed in tattered cords today, but in light-colored pants and a pale blue shirt that made his skin look very tan and his eyes very blue.

"You again!" he said in horror. "Leave it to you!"

"What did I do?" Toni asked, wondering if he was maybe a little crazy.

"You pressed the Up button when I told you not to," he said angrily.

"I usually do press the Up button when I want to go up," Toni said warily, moving to the far side of the elevator and deciding that he might really be mentally unbalanced.

"But I'd already pressed Down," he said, as if he were explaining something to a kindergartner.

"I don't see what the problem is," Toni said hesitantly. "If you pressed Down first, it will go down first."

Brandt shook his head. "Other elevators do that," he said. "This one is not like other elevators. If you press Down and then you press Up, it will go nowhere."

"Oh," Toni said, beginning to realize what he was saying, "You mean the elevator won't move?"

"Right."

"Then we'd better get out."

"How?"

Toni looked at the shut door. She looked at the panel of buttons. There were only two: Up and Down.

"There's no button to open the door," she said in a small voice.

"Right," he said again.

"So we're trapped in here?"

"Right again."

"Oh," Toni said. "We'd better call someone."

"In case you hadn't noticed," Brandt said sweetly, "there's no phone in this elevator. There also is no alarm button. Until someone else wants to use the elevator and it doesn't come, nobody will know we're here."

"Oh," Toni said.

"And don't keep saying 'oh,'" Brandt snapped.

"What else do you want me to say?" Toni demanded, "that I'm going to commit hara-kiri because I've stepped on your toes again?"

For the first time she saw his eyes flicker with amusement. "That wouldn't help in our present situation," he said. "In fact, without knowing it, you have probably succeeded in single-handedly wrecking my play." He leaned against the wall of the elevator and eyed her suspiciously. "Tell me honestly," he said, "were you sent here by some rival theater group to make sure that our play doesn't go on and that I will never get my first chance as a real director? Because if you were, you're doing a great job. . . . First you almost get me arrested. That would've looked wonderful in the papers and probably would've made the old fogies on the board of directors decide to fire me on the spot. And now you get me trapped in an elevator just when I should be meeting with Mr. Stanmore. Mr. Stanmore is on the board of directors of the Theater Alliance, by the way."

"I'm sorry," Toni said, looking at the floor of the elevator. "I don't really think I'm the cause of all of your problems, but I'll say I'm sorry if it makes you feel any better. Do you want me to grovel at your feet and beg forgiveness? That usually makes people feel pretty good."

She raised her eyes, saw the twinkle in his, and grinned at him.

"So you work up in the office, do you?" he asked, trying not to return her grin. "What's your name?"

"Toni. And I probably won't be working up in the office much longer when I show up over an hour late for work. Mrs. Thompson is only giving me a trial period."

"The old dragon is on your case, is she?" he asked, smiling down at her.

"She terrifies me," Toni admitted. "Whenever I do something wrong, she always seems to appear magically behind me."

"Don't worry, she terrifies everybody—me included," Brandt said. "And I probably won't be working here much longer, either, after Adriana spreads her side of the story around. We could go on welfare together, want to?—or maybe not. With my luck, you'd probably make something go wrong there, too. They'd decide I had to pay the government money, or they'd find me a job cleaning out pigsties . . . !" He sank to the floor, sitting with his back against the wall of the elevator. "This has been the worst week of my life," he said. "I am so tired."

As he sat there with his head in his hands, he looked just like a lost little boy. Toni noticed one tuft of hair that stuck up at the back of his head. For some reason it was very appealing. She squatted down beside him. "Did Adriana really walk out?" she asked after a long silence.

Brandt nodded. "She walked out," he said.

"I thought you were about to throw her out, anyway," Toni said.

Brandt sighed. "That was just a threat. I wanted to get her to shape up. It usually works . . ."

"So what's going to happen?" Toni asked after a long pause. "Don't you have an understudy?"

Brandt sighed again. "The understudy is fifty-five years old and, shall we say, a little heavy. You cannot have a fifty-five-year-old mermaid. The audience isn't supposed to burst into laughter when they see her draped over a rock!"

Toni giggled. "How did you come up with a fifty-five-year-old understudy?" she asked.

"Because this is amateur theater," Brandt said bitterly. "Everyone said, 'But Cora Dawson always has a part in our plays . . . ,' and there was no part for Cora Dawson. So I made her general understudy. How was I to know that someone was actually going to walk out on me?"

There was another long silence. Brandt stared at the floor. Toni looked down at his shoes and noticed how long and slim his feet were.

"I never should have taken this job," he muttered at last. "They warned me in college. 'Don't work with amateurs if you can help it,' they kept telling us. But I thought this would be different. I'd heard how professional this group was and how they often used professional actors for leading roles. It seemed like such a great first job . . . Now I know why all my friends are waiting tables or working in gas stations, waiting for their big break. It's less stressful, that's why."

"Is the play going to fall apart, then?" Toni asked cautiously.

"I don't know," Brandt said. "I'd sure hate to see all that hard work going down the drain. I just don't know how I'm going to replace Adriana. . . . Not that she could ever act to start with, stupid airhead! Just because she looked helpless and had blond hair didn't mean she could play a comedy role. Even when she got the lines right, which always seemed like a miracle, her timing was so bad that she ended up saying them over someone else's line. And she's supposed to be a future star. . . . Heaven help the future, that's what I say."

He looked up at Toni and smiled. "Is it my imagination, or is it getting hot in here?" he asked, wiping his hand across his face.

"It is getting a little stuffy," Toni agreed. "How many hours of oxygen do you think we have left?"

"Don't start talking like that—the last thing we want to do is panic. You breathe faster when you panic. Let's try to be calm and rational about this whole thing."

"Okay," Toni said. "I'm calm and rational. There's nothing to be scared about. Pam and Judy are working upstairs. At the very latest, they'll want to use the elevator to go home tonight, and then they'll discover it's not working and call somebody."

"What time do they usually go home?"

"Between five and six."

"That's at least four hours away! Do you think elevators hold four hours of oxygen?"

"Now who's panicking?"

"You brought it up. I'd never have thought of the oxygen giving out if you hadn't mentioned it!" Brandt got to his feet and began pacing up and down.

"Don't pace," Toni said sharply. "I'm sure you breathe more when you pace."

"I need to pace. I just won't breathe while I do it, okay?"

He walked to one wall of the elevator, thumped on it, and walked back again.

"Do you think anyone will hear us if we yell?" Toni asked.

"I don't know," he said. "We're a long way down from the office and there's nobody in the theater right now. We might use up precious oxygen yelling our lungs out for nothing."

"We could try one big thumping and yelling effort," Toni suggested.

"Okay. We'll try," Brandt agreed. "Ready, get set, go." Toni began banging on the door, while Brandt hit the walls, yelling "Help! Get us out of here, we're trapped! Help."

After a minute they stopped, exhausted.

"It's no use," Toni said hopelessly. "Nobody heard us."

"We used up precious oxygen for nothing," Brandt said.

"It was my idea—why don't you go ahead and blame me for it?" Toni asked. "That would give you one more thing to add to the list."

Brandt sank down to the elevator floor again. When he looked up at her, Toni noticed that his blue eyes were fringed with thick, dark lashes. "I don't blame you, Toni," he said. "In fact, I don't hold the other things against you, either. They were only accidents. I know you didn't mean any harm. I don't want to die without saying that to you . . ."

"I don't want to die, period," Toni said, sitting down next to him. "We're not going to die. What kind of defeatist talk is that? Someone will come and rescue us. Pam and Judy will go home. . . . People will come for rehearsal . . ."

"I've been thinking about that," Brandt said. "What if Pam and Judy just decide the elevator isn't working and go down the fire escape? What if they weren't even in the office today? Is anybody going to miss you this evening? If I don't show up for rehearsal, everyone will think I'm just sulking about Adriana. Nobody may use the side entrance until tomorrow, and by then it may be too late . . ."

"Oh, shut up," Toni said. "Maybe someone will decide to drop the bomb on Seattle during the night, too. Maybe there'll be a tidal wave and we'll drown . . ."

"We'd survive a tidal wave," Brandt said, giving her a weak grin. "If no oxygen can get in, then water certainly can't either."

"So we have one comforting thought," Toni said. "At least we can't be drowned before morning."

"You know, you're a pretty gutsy person," Brandt said. "Most girls I know would be clinging to me and crying by now."

"I never cling," Toni said. "And I hardly ever cry, either."

"Tough cookie, eh?"

Toni shook her head. "Not really," she said. "I just don't like to show it when I'm scared."

"And are you scared right now?" he asked gently.

Toni nodded.

"Me, too."

"There's one good thing about this, though," Toni said, looking up at him with a little smile. "If we're both found dead in the elevator, it'll be terrific publicity for your play."

"Thanks a lot," Brandt said, grinning back at her. "Somehow right now that thought is not very comforting."

"I'm just trying to keep our spirits up," Toni said. She wiped her hand across her forehead. "It sure is getting hot in here," she said.

"You're right," Brandt agreed, and he started to unbutton his shirt.

Toni noticed that he didn't have a T-shirt underneath his blue button-down. "It's great for you," Toni said. "I can't take off my sweatshirt!"

"Don't mind me," Brandt said, flinging his shirt in the corner. "I don't care, and if they're only going to find our bodies, anyway, who cares what you're wearing?"

"Thanks a lot," Toni snapped. "If my dead body is going to be found, I prefer it to be properly clothed, thank you."

Brandt laughed. "Maybe we should stop talking so much," he said. "We should try to relax and conserve oxygen." He moved closer to her. "Funny the way things turn out, isn't it?"

Toni noticed the taut muscles in his arms and chest as he shifted his body to a more comfortable position. "You don't really think we're going to die, do you?" she asked in a small voice.

"No. Someone is bound to find us," Brandt said gently. He put his arm around Toni. She shuddered. "Don't worry. We'll get out. Someone will come. . . . And this dilapidated old elevator . . . I bet it has enough cracks in it to let in just enough air . . ."

"Then why do I feel so sleepy?" Toni asked, closing her eyes. Her head sank onto Brandt's shoulder.

Suddenly Toni opened her eyes. She'd heard a noise! As she stared straight ahead, the elevator door slowly opened. Mrs. Thompson stood in the doorway. She took one look at Brandt and Toni, slumped together on the floor—Brandt with his bare chest, Toni nestled against his shoulder.

"What *is* going on in here?" she demanded.

TEN

Dear Jill,

I hope this letter hurries and gets to you because I can't wait another minute to tell you. I have just met the most wonderful, terrific, exciting guy in the entire world. He's the director of our play at the theater. He's twenty-one and has just gotten out of UCLA, where he specialized in directing. He is tall and kind of skinny, but not too skinny. Lean, I think you would call it, and he has a terrific tan from living in Los Angeles and his hair is all sun-streaked at the front and he has very blue eyes. What's more, he lives for the theater and he has a terrible temper, just like me.

Don't we sound perfect for each other? There's only one small obstacle to our future happiness. . . . He's not exactly in love with me. In fact, he may well go out of his way to avoid me in the future, because I've brought him nothing but bad luck! First I almost got him arrested . . . and then I got us trapped in an elevator. . . . But that's a long story. I'll give you all the intimate details the next time I see you.

The bad part, in terms of my professional life, though, is that unfortunately the person who rescued us from the elevator was none other than Mrs. Thompson. She's been in a terrible mood because it looks as though the play might be canceled, so she wasn't too thrilled to find us. I think she decided we'd been having an orgy in her elevator! We both did look pretty disheveled—Brandt with no shirt on and me half asleep on his shoulder. Did I mention his name was Brandt—isn't that a nice, strong, masculine name? Anyway, Mrs. Thompson was horrible to Brandt. She said she hoped the play was going to be a big success after all the trouble it had caused and talked about the board reviewing his contract! She's like that—know what I mean? Rich people—they never come right out and say, 'I think you've really messed up.' They just act very sweet and drop hints, which is far worse. I expected her to hint around that I'd better look for another job, too, but I don't think she even was paying that much attention to me. She was more concerned with Brandt and the play, so I was able to slink away up the fire escape. He didn't even see me go because Mrs. Thompson had him firmly by the arm and was leading him down to the theater.

I've been thinking about him every minute since, Jill. In fact I missed my stop on the bus home and had to walk back two blocks in the dark. Not funny!! How can I ever get him to like me? I don't dare go down to the theater because, knowing me, I'll knock over some priceless antique lamp or something. Maybe there'll be a party after the play and the play will have gone well and Brandt will be feeling happy and I'll be there in my prettiest dress and he'll look across the room and notice me for the first time and . . . Do things like that ever happen in real life, Jill?

The big problem is that I don't seem to have confidence anymore. I'm very conscious that I'm a little kid straight out of high school and he's a mature adult who has finished college. How can I ever make Brandt think I'm an interesting person when there are gorgeous, talented, sophisticated women floating around? I wish my college had a course called Sophistication 1–2, or How to Grow Up in a Hurry.

Any ideas will be gratefully accepted. After all, you're something of an expert, having kept one good-looking boyfriend for more than a year. Did you two have a wonderful Sunday together after you left me? I was thinking of you both (and feeling a teeny bit jealous, if you want to know). I realize now that I did all the talking on

Saturday and I didn't really ask you about your life at all. I guess you caught me at a low point. But I won't ever be like that again—promise!—because now I have HOPE. I can dream about Brandt every spare minute. So write me a really long letter and tell me everything that's happened to you.

I went home on Sunday to raid our kitchen . . . well, officially, to see my parents. The kitchen raiding was unofficial. My dad seems a lot livelier already. He even promised to come and fix the legs on my furniture soon if the doctor gives him the go-ahead. I came back with two huge boxes of stuff—all essential to survival, like a little heater, a can opener that works, a pot holder (you burn yourself grabbing TV dinners with your bare hands), a frying pan and another pot (no more spaghetti and sauce cooked together), the comforter for my bed, a knife that cuts, and hundreds of little things you never think of until you need them—things like salt or matches or detergent—do you realize that apartments need cleaning? I had overlooked that fact until I put something down on my counter yesterday and it stuck to it. I'm going to have to find an old vacuum cleaner, too, because the dust is breeding in my rug. My parents wouldn't let me take theirs—nor their washing machine or dishwasher. Don't you think that's mean of them? I have to keep the place looking good from now on, just in case Brandt ever comes around. You never know, he might offer me a ride home in the rain one night and I might invite him up for a cup of coffee and . . .

Dream on, Toni! At least I have something to dream about again! I'm beginning to feel alive for the first time since we got back from Europe. I hope I'll be writing to you soon with good news. If the news is that good, I may even splurge and phone!

Have fun, Jill.

Luv, luv, luv, Toni.

Toni was finding it very hard to concentrate at work. Knowing that Brandt was in the same building, just separated from her by one set of floorboards and yet completely out of reach, made any logical thinking impossible. Every time she stared down at the white sheet of paper in her typewriter, a suntanned face with bright blue eyes and long eyelashes shimmered above the typed letters. Every time she heard a man's voice outside the window or a heavy step down the hall, her heart leaped alarmingly.

"You're so jumpy today," Pam commented. "Is something wrong?"

"No, nothing, why?" Toni asked, trying to keep her voice even and pretending to concentrate on her filing.

"Because you almost shut that file on your fingertips when I opened the door," Pam said, smiling. "I'm beginning to think you must have a guilty secret."

"Maybe she's waiting for a phone call from her boyfriend," Judy suggested, smiling at Toni. Toni felt herself blushing like a little kid. "See, what did I tell you?" Judy said, laughing. "I can always tell when someone's in love. I remember how I used to be—back in the good old days before diapers and ear infections and broken garbage disposals!"

Pam sighed. "It seems so long ago, doesn't it?" she asked. "You're so lucky, Toni. You have the exciting part of your life ahead of you."

"I hope it gets a little more exciting than it's been recently," Toni said, closing the file drawer with a bang. To change the subject she picked up a sheet of paper from Judy's desk. "Oh, is this the program design? It's really nice."

"Yes, it's not bad, is it?" Judy said. "Would you make us some copies so that we can send them out to the board for approval?"

"Sure," Toni said, glad to escape to the little back room with the copying machine, where Pam and Judy couldn't watch her every move or ask anymore questions. The copying machine whirred loudly while she ran off ten copies. As she turned it off again, she became aware of another person speaking in the next room. "So they told me the printer was going to make the changes and . . ." the person was saying. The very familiar voice made her stop for a moment. Toni peeped through the crack in the door of the back room and saw Brandt standing in the office doorway, one hand casually resting on the door frame. He looked even more wonderful than he had yesterday.

Act cool, you idiot, she commanded herself silently. *Don't let him see you blushing. Remember: you're an efficient secretary!* She swept across the office and gave him a beaming smile. "I'll bet you came up to see this," she said, waving the sheet confidently at him. "This is the Brandt that arrived from the program. I mean, the designs that changed the printer. . . . No, the printeds you designed from the . . ." Toni's voice stumbled to a halt. She handed him the sheet, blushing furiously, and fled across to her desk. She was all too aware of three sets of eyes, all watching her. All looking amused.

Why do I always have to blow it? she screamed at herself. *My big chance, and I blew it. Now he'll always think of me as an idiot!* She didn't dare look up, and pretended to be very busy finding something in her desk drawer.

"Anything else you need while you're here, Brandt?" Pam asked.

"I just got a great idea," he said. "Toni?"

Toni hardly dared look up, but she did.

"Could you spare a moment to come with me?" he asked.

"What for?" Toni stammered.

"Something I want to try out."

Toni got to her feet. She knew very well she would have gone with him if he'd led her into a tank of man-eating sharks. "You want me to test an elevator for you?" she managed to say with a weak grin.

He shook his head. "Uh-uh. Never again will I get into an elevator with you!" he declared, smiling. "We'll go down the fire escape, and I want you to go first so you don't fall on me!"

"Where are we going?" Toni asked as they started to clatter down the iron steps.

"Just down to the theater."

"What for?"

"I want you to try something."

That's it, Toni thought. *He's got some sort of trapdoor or flying mechanism or something dangerous in the play and he wants to try it out on me before he risks any member of the cast in it.* She felt stupidly disappointed. For one absurd moment she had dreamed that he might actually have been inviting her somewhere exciting—out for coffee in the little café around the corner, where they would sit and talk at that intimate table in the corner . . .

"In here," Brandt said, opening the door for her. "Watch your step backstage, there are cables lying around all over the place." Brandt went ahead and looked around. "Leon?" he called.

"Down here."

"Come up here, will you? I've got a great idea I want to show you."

A big man with sagging jowls and a lot of graying hair poked his head out from under the stage. "What great idea now?" he growled.

"Watch," Brandt said. "Here, Toni—this is what I want you to try for me. I want you to walk in through that door, across to this chair, and say these lines. Can you do that?"

"I guess so," Toni said, wondering what the trick was. She stood behind the scenery door and waited. "Now?" she asked.

"Now," Brandt said. Toni looked at the door but it had no handle. She pushed at it but it didn't move.

"You can come in now," Brandt called impatiently.

"I can't open the door," Toni yelled back.

"Give it a good push," Brandt shouted. Toni thought she could hear him laughing. She hurled herself against the door. It came flying open and she was propelled onto the set, staggering past the sofa, and almost knocking over a side table with a lamp on it.

"I'm sorry," she called. "The door opened so suddenly. Do you want me to do it again?"

"No, that was perfect," Brandt said. She could hear his laughter clearly now. "Say the lines."

Toni looked down. "Goodness, I'll never get the hang of doors," she said. "Or of legs for that matter."

106

Brandt and Leon both laughed loudly. Toni looked up suspiciously, wondering what trick they were playing on her.

"Well, what do you think, Leon?" Brandt asked. "Isn't she just perfect?"

"Perfect," Leon agreed. "I think you've solved our problems, kid. Where did you find her?"

"Upstairs in the office," Brandt said. "She's a natural if ever I saw one."

Toni looked from one face to the other. "Would somebody please tell me what's going on?" she asked.

"Congratulations, kid," Leon said. "How would you like to play a mermaid?"

"In the play, you mean?" Toni stammered.

Brandt smiled at her. "I don't mean in the ocean," he said, "I mean take over Adriana's part. The part was just made for you. You'll have to work very hard because we have less than two weeks to rehearse, but I think you could do it. What do you say, Toni? Will you save our play for us?"

Don't pinch me, anybody, because I don't want to wake up, Toni thought. She took a deep breath. "I have always wanted to sit on a rock, combing my hair," she said.

ELEVEN

Playing the mermaid was the most exciting thing that had ever happened to Toni. She'd had the lead in the school musical the year before, but that had just been high-school kids and sets made of cardboard. This was the real thing—a big stage with real actors, complicated lighting cues, costumes designed by a New York designer, and, for Toni, the most gorgeous long blond wig.

If Toni was thrilled to get the part, the rest of the performers and stage personnel were equally delighted with her. Even Brandt had had no idea what a quick study Toni was. He had guessed she'd look and sound right, but he was amazed at the speed with which she learned her lines.

"You really are a natural," he'd said, beaming at her delightedly. "You're going to be terrific in this part."

Toni even overheard the distinguished-looking man who played the millionaire fisherman who catches the mermaid from his boat saying, "What a clever little actress."

Suddenly it seemed that Toni was "somebody"—and that felt very good. Up in the office she was no longer the person Friday, the girl you asked to make you more coffee or run off some copies. She was, according to Mrs. Thompson, *our* leading lady." She still did the same work, but she could tell that they now thought she was somebody special.

In bed at night she would run over in her mind that wonderful scene when Brandt had broken the news to the others. They had all been there—Pam and Judy standing behind Mrs. Thompson while she went over the seating plan with them. They had looked up when Toni and Brandt came in.

"Oh, Toni, you're back, dear," Mrs. Thompson had said. "That's good. I've some letters we must get out today. . . . Was there something you needed, Brandt?"

"I just came up to make an announcement," Brandt had said. "I thought you might be relieved to know that we have found a new mermaid."

"Oh, thank heavens for that," Mrs. Thompson had sighed. "Is she any good?"

"She's going to be terrific."

"What's her name—do I know her?" Mrs. Thompson had asked.

"You know her pretty well," Brandt had said, while Toni felt a blush beginning to suffuse her cheeks. "It's Toni here."

Three pairs of eyes had all stared at her as if Brandt had just announced that she was a mass murderer or a Russian spy.

"Toni?" Mrs. Thompson had stammered, actually losing her cool for a couple of seconds. "Toni?"

"That's right," Brandt had said. "She's perfect for the part. She's going to do it very well."

"But I had no idea . . ." Mrs. Thompson had stuttered.

"Oh, yes, she's a very experienced actress," Brandt had said smoothly. "She just doesn't like to boast about her achievements."

Toni had stifled a grin and tried to look like a star who doesn't boast. The three faces that stared at her were a picture of confusion.

"I can't wait to see you in the part, Toni," Mrs. Thompson had said, hinting that Toni would probably be terrible and she would be able to prove Brandt wrong.

"I think that's wonderful, Toni," Pam had said.

"And you're very brave to take on such a big part on such short notice," Judy had added. "You'll have to work incredibly hard learning all those lines."

"Don't worry, I'm going to work hard," Toni had said.

Word had spread around quickly that Toni was good in the part, and pretty soon Mrs. Thompson had shown up for rehearsal to see for herself. She must have been impressed, because she started calling Toni "our leading lady" right after that. Much to Toni's embarrassment, she used it as a boast to other people.

"The programs?" she would say over the phone. "Our leading lady is taking care of them herself. Isn't that sweet of her? Such a modest person and such a good actress, too . . ."

In fact, everything in Toni's world was perfect, except that Brandt was still being just a director and not showing any signs of being interested in her as a person. She saw him every evening, but all the time she was just one of the cast, to be yelled at if she made a wrong move and praised if she got something right. When he came and stood close to her, showing her something he wanted done, Toni tingled all over. Sometimes he touched her, shifting her position on the rock or adjusting her tail, and Toni felt as if she had gotten an electric shock. But when she sneaked a quick look at Brandt's face, it seemed that he hadn't felt a thing.

At least he hasn't mentioned a girlfriend, she tried to cheer herself up by thinking. *So far no girls have shown up on the set. At least there's still hope.*

In fact, she spent all her spare time hoping, trying to think of ways to make him fall in love with her. Not that she had much spare time anymore. When she got up in the morning, she recited lines out loud to herself while she showered, dressed and ate breakfast. She chanted lines as she walked toward college. Through all her classes she had become pretty skilled at having the play open between sheets of business math and English. She read lines on the bus to work, usually eating a piece of fruit, or a Twinkie on the days when her willpower was weak. Then, after working in the office for five or six hours, she went straight down to the theater.

At first she didn't even notice her tiredness, because everything was so exciting. But after a few days it hit her. The rehearsals began to go on longer and longer. When scene rehearsals had finished, the actors had to wait around for technical rehearsals, walking across the stage ten times to get the spotlighting correct.

"Are you still with us, Toni?" Brandt asked sharply one night when he'd given an instruction and everyone else had moved to the other side of the stage to start the scene over.

"Oh, er, sorry, Brandt," Toni mumbled.

"Then pay attention," he growled. "I don't want to have to say everything twice for your benefit. We have a lot to get through, and you're holding us all up."

Toni opened her mouth to say that there wouldn't be any play without her and that he should be proud that she didn't need her script, but then she remembered that this was Brandt—the one person in the world she wanted to like her. She swallowed hard. "Okay, Brandt," she said, going to join the others.

For the rest of the evening she fought her tiredness, doing aerobic jumps and head circles to keep her blood circulating between scenes. Then

Brandt called for the bathtub scene, the scene in which the millionaire comes in to take a shower and finds the mermaid in his bath. It was one of the funniest scenes in the play. Toni lowered herself into the tub for the opening of the scene. The stage manager helped arrange her tail and adjusted her hair. Of course, there was no water in the tub. The stage manager had told Toni that on opening night there would be a bubble machine behind her, but during rehearsals just a plain, empty tub was used.

Toni lay in the tub in the darkness and closed her eyes. Only one more scene and she could go home . . . wonderful soft bed, sleep for eight hours . . .

"Toni!" She felt a hand on her arm and opened her eyes in alarm. She was going to be late for her first class, she'd better hurry . . .

She tried to get up and found that she couldn't move. For some reason her legs were tied together. She looked down at the long, silver tail, then up at the person beside her. Suddenly she remembered where she was.

"Oh, Brandt, I'm so sorry," she mumbled. "I must have fallen asleep."

"So I noticed," he said.

"I'm ready now. We can begin the scene again," Toni said anxiously.

Brandt's face softened into a smile. "There's nobody here," he said. "They've all gone home."

Toni attempted to sit up. "I've been asleep that long?" she stammered.

"About half an hour," he said, perching on the tub beside her.

"Oh, no." Toni pushed at her hair in embarrassment, but only succeeded in shoving the wig to one side. "I'm sorry," she muttered, trying to straighten the wig. "I really didn't mean to. It's just that it was dark and . . ."

"It's okay," Brandt said. "I understand. I didn't realize before how incredibly hard you must have been working. You got all those lines down in a couple of days. You're trying to fit in college and a job and this. I would've collapsed days ago. Come on, I'll help you off with your tail."

They both giggled as he pulled and she wriggled until he staggered backward, sitting down with the huge silver tail flopped on top of him.

"I'm going to stick to sardines in the future," he muttered, scrambling to his feet while Toni laughed. "Come on, let's get out of here." He reached down to her, took both her hands, and lifted her to her feet.

"I'm so embarrassed about falling asleep," Toni said as she put the wig back on its stand and ran a brush through her curls. "The others must think I'm a complete weirdo."

"They think you're pretty good," Brandt said. "They were all very impressed with how quickly you got into the part. And they know damn well that

114

you saved their play. You should have seen them tiptoe out when I sent them home." He smiled at Toni. "I couldn't decide whether to let you sleep there all night or wake you and take you home. Then I thought you'd have a very stiff neck in the morning if you slept all night in a bathtub. I did that once after a really wild party in college. I don't recommend it. But you got off lucky. The way they woke me up was by turning on the cold-water faucet!"

As he talked they walked together up the center aisle to the back of the theater. Toni waited while he turned out the lights, then they walked out to the front of the building.

"Do you have a car?" he asked.

"Are you kidding? On my salary I can barely afford to eat," Toni said, laughing.

"Then I'll give you a ride home," he said. "I'm parked just around the corner. On second thought—if you can hardly afford to eat, I'll bet you haven't had dinner yet. You want to come have something? I'm starving, myself. I know this place that stays open very late and serves super Italian food."

"Sounds great," Toni said, suddenly feeling very wide awake and very hungry.

They drove down the waterfront to Mario's Restaurant. The outside didn't look like much—an old brick building with a gaudy neon sign, but once she walked in through the doors, Toni got a shock.

In front of her was a huge room, full of round tables covered in red checkered tablecloths and lit only by candles in wax-covered wine bottles. There were hanging plants overhead, and soft Italian music was playing. Couples at tables were sipping wine. A waiter came over and led Brandt and Toni to a table in a corner. Toni glanced around nervously.

"Is something wrong?" Brandt asked.

Toni grinned. "It's just that I've never been in a place like this before."

Brandt looked surprised. "You make it sound like a strip joint or something."

"It's just so grown-up and elegant," Toni said. "I feel like I don't belong here somehow . . ."

"Well, for your information," Brandt said smoothly, "you are now grown-up and elegant. You can eat wherever you want to. In fact, I wouldn't be surprised if the next time you come in here everyone whisper's, 'Look, that's Toni Redmond—the new star of that play, directed by that brilliant young director—what's his name?'"

Toni laughed. "Fat chance," she said.

"You never know," Brandt said. "This may be your big break. A lot of important people come to our plays. Maybe the head of MGM will be front row, center, on opening night—or someone from Broadway and they'll ask you to take over the lead in a new play and you'll win a Tony award and . . ."

"You're teasing me," Toni said. "That's not fair."

Brandt smiled. "Is that what you really dream for yourself?" he asked. "Is that what you want?"

"I wasn't really sure until now," Toni said, playing with her napkin under the tablecloth. "I always liked acting, but I thought of it as something you do for fun. I never thought I'd be good enough to make the real theater . . ."

"I think you could be," Brandt said. "Of course, you need training. But you have a really good sense of timing and comedy . . . and you're cute!"

"You're cute." His words sang through Toni's head. *He thinks I can be a real actress. I don't believe it!*

Their waiter returned and Brandt ordered the fettuccine, which was the restaurant's specialty. When it came Toni looked at the plate and thought that she would rather have had a good old, filling, helping of lasagna or even a pile of spaghetti and meatballs. The fettuccine was very delicate, with an herby flavor and a creamy sauce. She hoped she wouldn't starve to death. Still, she ate it politely, feeling very adult and listening to Brandt tell her about the theater program at UCLA.

"You might think about UCLA for yourself," he said. "It's about the best place you can go."

Toni sighed. "I can't think of going away anywhere for a while," she said. "My father had a heart attack this summer and he can't go back to work yet. We don't know if he can ever work again. Until he's completely well I don't want to move away from Seattle, and I can't expect any money for college. Maybe I can keep saving and in my junior year . . ."

"Sure, why not," Brandt said encouragingly. "And in the meantime you can act in my plays and in plays at the college—not that the college plays will be up to my standard! Get as much experience as you can."

Toni was almost floating as they left the restaurant. Brandt wanted her in his plays—two whole years of working with him. During that time he'd have to like her better and better, until maybe, some day . . .

Halfway to the door they passed another couple coming in.

"Why, Brandt, darling, surprise, surprise," a smooth voice said. For a second Toni couldn't remember who the beautiful blond girl was, but then she heard Brandt say, "Adriana! Surprise, indeed."

"I must congratulate you on your persistence, darling," Adriana said evenly. "I hear that you're still plodding along with your little play."

"That's it," Brandt said pleasantly, "still plodding along."

"Why don't you just admit defeat, darling?" Adriana asked. "It won't do you any good to direct a flop."

"Who says it's going to be a flop, Adriana?" Brandt asked. "Actually, I think it's going to be pretty damn good."

Adriana laughed. She had a wonderful, musical laugh. "But, darling—I heard you were so desperate for a new mermaid that you had to use one of the office girls."

"Best thing that ever happened," Brandt said, "because she turned out to be much better than you."

"I can understand that, darling," Adriana said poisonously, "because the part calls for a dumb klutz. So she wouldn't have to stretch her acting ability very far, would she?"

Toni had been heating up to the boiling point. There was a large plate of spaghetti bolognese on the table behind Adriana, and Toni felt very tempted to push her backward into it. She had a wonderful vision of Adriana with her legs sticking up in the air while she fought to stand up again and bolognese sauce soaking into her pink dress. But at the same time a little voice inside Toni's head whispered that this wasn't the way civilized adults behaved and if she wanted to be treated like an adult, she'd better behave like one. She decided to fight Adriana at her own game instead. She stepped out from behind Brandt.

"Well, darling, *your* acting ability couldn't be stretched across a trapeze at a flea circus," she said.

Toni had a loud voice and several people at nearby tables smiled. Adriana's face turned pink. She seemed to notice Toni for the first time. She looked at her as if she were a cockroach that had just crawled out from under the table.

"Are you the little girl he found in the office? How sweet—I'm sure you're just perfect for the part of the dumb blond. But you must tell me your name. . . . I don't think we've met before."

"Oh, but we have met before," Toni said, just as sweetly. "Don't you remember? I had to call the triple A for you when you locked your keys in your car. Not at all the sort of thing a dumb blond would do—why, that would take a total airhead!"

"You little . . ." Adriana stuttered. "You forget who you're talking to."

"No, I remember very well who I'm talking to," Toni said. "You were the one who forgot . . . because I was a nobody then." She turned to Brandt. "Come on, Brandt, let's go. We're wasting our time here."

"It's very clear how you got the part, darling," Adriana called to Toni's back. "By chasing the director! We've all heard about the casting couch."

Brandt looked back and laughed. "If you want to know the truth, Adriana—not only did she chase me—she trapped me in an elevator and kept me there for two hours! That's the kind of girl I like— one with guts. Oh, and she makes a great mermaid, too—you should see her in the bathtub." He grabbed Toni's arm and they both ran out, laughing.

"Toni, you were terrific," Brandt said. He grabbed her shoulders and pulled her toward him.

He towered over her, laughing down at her. "I'm discovering new things about you every minute. I had no idea you could squash someone like Adriana so beautifully. I nearly died laughing."

Toni could feel his hands, warm and strong, through her sweater. Her heart was hammering so hard that she could hardly breathe.

"You were pretty good yourself," she said. "She was trying so hard to make you lose your cool."

"It takes a lot to make me lose my cool," Brandt said. "In fact, it takes something like standing alone in the dark with a pretty girl in my arms . . ."

There was a long pause. Toni could see his eyes sparkling in the light of the neon sign.

"Even when you trapped me in that elevator I thought you were cute," Brandt said at last in a low voice. "I thought to myself, if you have to be trapped with anyone then this isn't half bad. And back then I didn't know that you were smart and talented and fun as well as cute. In fact now I could kick myself that we wasted all that time alone together . . ."

"We talked a lot," Toni whispered.

"But who wants to talk?" Brandt whispered back.

"You're talking right now," Toni teased, her eyes laughing into his.

"I just finished," he said, his lips meeting hers.

TWELVE

Toni!

I was so excited for you when I got your phone call. I don't know if I understood everything you said—you tend to babble when you get excited—but I think what you were trying to tell me is that you have the lead in the play and you and Brandt are an item! That's really too much good news for one person to have at one time—you're taking more than your share, Toni Redmond. How about your poor friend down at Rosemont, plodding along in her lonely life? . . . Of course I don't really mean that. I'm thrilled for you, Toni. It's about time things started to go well for you. I was worried about you when I was down for the weekend because you were so depressed, and I didn't know what to say to make you feel better. Obviously I didn't need to say anything because great things were waiting for you just around the corner.

Of course I'll come up and see the play! I had promised myself that I wouldn't spend any more money coming home this whole semester, but I can't miss my best friend in her first starring role. I can't wait to see you as a mermaid. I hope they've given you enough hair—and that the wig doesn't fall off at the wrong moment! Also I can't wait to see Brandt. He sounds like a wonderful guy!

I don't know about bringing Craig with me, or the foursome for dinner afterward. It's sort of complicated . . . Things aren't going smoothly in that department. I'll tell you all about it when I see you—if you're not too busy being famous.

Nothing much has happened in college since I talked to you last. Robert and I are freshmen reps for the literary magazine. At the rate poems and stories are coming in, I think we might have to write half the magazine ourselves. Robert writes very good poetry—very satirical with a bite to it. His poems make my nature poems seem very wishy-washy, although Robert says they're good. Charles (the weird one) came into my room last night with a very odd poem—about ten pages long and rambling—all about death. He stayed to talk so long we had to throw him out in the end. I feel sorry for him, but he definitely is weird. He's so intense—he stands very close to you and breathes down at you—Cassie says he gives her the creeps. He does me, too, but I know he needs friends, so I can't always send him away. I think he may be in love with me. It's nice to know that somebody is, but I do wish it weren't Charles!

Must stop now. I have two papers due tomorrow. Why don't teachers ever check with one another before they hand out assignments? They all think that theirs is the only class in the world that matters.

If I don't see you before the show goes on, then break a leg—isn't that what they say? But don't knock over any furniture with your tail—how do you move in it, anyway? I'm dying to see.

Love, Jill.

Jill!!

Soo glad you're coming! You have to come up to my dressing room before I go on. I'll need all the support I can get. I'm just beginning to realize I'm in a real play and lots of real people will be watching me and there are so many chances for things to go wrong! I have to cross that stage in a tail several times, luckily carried by someone else, but one wrong move of that appendage and I could sweep a precious antique lamp to the floor. And you know how good I am at making wrong moves! I woke up last night sweating after a bad dream in which I lost control of my tail and destroyed the entire set! Brandt is so sweet. He says that even top actors have opening night nerves. Those dumb people in college, though, don't have any idea about what's going on. I asked to be excused from a business math test because of opening night and do you know what the teacher said? She said, 'We must get our priorities right, mustn't we, Toni? After all, college work has to come before our hobbies if we want to succeed in life!' To her, success in life is getting a good job in a boring office. Just wait until I'm a success in the theater—I'll sweep into her class and tell her just what I think of her!

Must go. About to go crazy trying to fit everything into one life of twenty-four-hour days. . . . PLEASE be there before the show, Jill. I need you.

Luv, Toni.

The backstage area of the theater was certainly not glamorous. Racks of dresses and old pieces of scenery stacked in the hallway made it almost impossible to squeeze past to the dressing rooms. Toni's dressing room was tucked away between a broom closet and two towering pillars from the Roman Empire. Jill knocked lightly on the door and went in.

"Jill, thank heavens you're here," Toni said from a chair in the corner.

"Toni—is that really you under all that hair?" Jill asked, laughing delightedly. "And what an enormous tail. I had no idea it was so huge. How on earth do you move around with that thing on?"

"I don't," Toni said. "That's why I'm so glad to see you. I was beginning to panic. Someone was supposed to come and help me down to the stage for Act One and nobody's shown up. I thought I'd have to drag myself down the hall and I wouldn't make it on time and Act One would start without me and I'd be all covered with dust and my tail would be all ripped . . ."

Jill walked over to Toni and put a hand on her shoulder. "Will you calm down," she said. "There are still ten minutes until the play starts. You have plenty of time. If nobody shows up, I'll help you."

"But you can't carry me, Jill—how am I going to get down the hall?"

"Toni—relax! I'll find someone to help me. Okay?"

"But what if you can't find anybody?"

"Then I'll round up the coffee cart and push you along on that! Stop panicking, will you?"

"But I'm supposed to be onstage by now. I always was in dress rehearsals. I hate it when things go wrong. What if that's a sign that nothing's going to go smoothly tonight? What if I knock things over and forget my lines and I'm a big flop and everyone is mad at Brandt for choosing me and he's mad at me because they're all mad at him . . ."

"And a Martian spaceship lands and wipes out beautiful downtown Seattle? You're funny, Toni.

Everything's going to be terrific. Remember the high-school musical, how nervous you got beforehand and then you were fantastic?"

"Yeah," Toni said, looking up and smiling for the first time. "I did get pretty nervous then, didn't I?"

"Nervous? You drove everyone out of their minds! We had to check every stitch in your costume to reassure you it wasn't going to fall down onstage—I had to spray your throat three times in case you got tonsillitis during the overture, and I had to wave my own copy of the script at you, in case you forgot your lines and the prompter had fallen asleep."

"It wasn't that bad," Toni said, "but I can't help being nervous. You can imagine what it's like, sitting in here all alone, unable to move, wondering if the rest of the cast is already onstage and nobody will come for me . . ."

"Well, they can hardly start without you," Jill said, laughing. "There wouldn't be much of a story without the mermaid, would there? They'd have to scratch out half the title: *The Millionaire and*—that's not nearly as catchy!"

Toni managed a giggle. "You're crazy," she said. "I'm glad you're here. I feel better already."

"I almost didn't make it," Jill said. "I thought I'd save some money by getting a ride with a group of kids driving up for a soccer game. I thought it was a real smart idea until I saw their car."

"Toni grinned. "Sounds like something I'd do. Go on. What was wrong with the car?"

"It was a fifties Chevy—you know, big fins, glaring chrome. And seven kids were packed into it. The engine sounded as if it hadn't been tuned since the fifties."

Toni laughed out loud.

"It broke down four times on the way up—and I had to run the last two blocks to the theater." Jill started to laugh. "And then I was so out of breath, I couldn't even tell the man at the door who I was so he'd let me in and I just pushed past him and ran back here."

They were both still giggling when the door opened and Brandt came in.

"Where's my star mermaid?" he asked. "Time you were onstage!"

"I was waiting for someone to come and sweep me off my tail," Toni quipped.

"Like this?" he asked, scooping her up into his arms. Toni twined her arms around his neck. "Just like that," she said, gazing up at him adoringly.

"Okay, let's go, my little sardine," he said, giving her a light peck on the lips. "It's all right. I didn't smudge your makeup."

For the moment Jill had been forgotten. Then Toni remembered her friend. "Oh, Brandt," she said, "I almost forgot. This is my best friend, Jill Gardner. She's come all the way from Oregon, just for opening night."

Brandt turned and beamed at Jill. "Glad to meet you," he said. "Excuse us if we run right now. We've got a date with a curtain that's about to go up, but I'll see you at the party afterward—okay?"

"Sure," Jill said. "See you then."

"'Bye, Jill," Toni called. "Cross your fingers for me, okay? I hope I don't blow it!"

"You'll be terrific, as always, Toni Redmond," Jill called. "Now get out there and wow 'em."

And Toni was terrific—from the first moment she appeared onstage, in a giant net at the back of the set. She was in command. At her first line, to the old man who'd caught her, "Well you're not much of a catch yourself!" the audience exploded with laughter. After that she enjoyed every minute onstage. The audience clearly loved her. She only had to say the most ordinary line and they all laughed and applauded. At one point, when a doorknob came off in her hand, which was supposed to happen, and at another when she fell off a chair, which wasn't, the audience roared. At the end of the play Toni accepted a standing ovation with tears of joy stinging in her eyes.

Right after the play Jill rushed into the dressing room. "Toni, you were wonderful," she said, hugging her friend.

"Yes, I was rather spectacular, darling, wasn't I?" Toni clowned. "Have any talent scouts from MGM been asking for me yet? Just tell them to wait and I'll have my agent negotiate with them later."

She turned back to her mirror and started taking off her makeup. "I'm so glad it's over, Jill. I was terrified."

"You were not," Jill said severely. "You were having a ball out there. I could tell!"

"I was terrified at the same time," Toni said, tossing a cotton ball into the wastebasket. "Good shot, Toni. I should sign up for basketball, don't you think?"

"Most basketball players are taller than five two," Jill said. "If I were you, I'd stick to acting. You'll make a lot more money."

"Do you really think so?" Toni asked. "Do you think I'm good enough to do this for money?"

"I thought you were great, Toni," Jill said seriously. "Your acting tonight was as good as anything I've seen in the movies!"

"The audience liked it, didn't they?" Toni asked hesitantly.

"They loved it. Why else do you think they gave you a standing ovation? And they laughed at every word you said!"

"They roared when I fell off that chair," Toni said sharply. "That wasn't in the script. Somebody moved that chair from its chalk mark, I swear it."

"Well, accident or not, I'd leave it in if I were you. Everyone loved it, and it was just right in that scene."

"It also hurt," Toni said, brushing at her hair savagely. "I don't know if I'm willing to sacrifice my tailbone for five more performances."

"Great comics have to take pratfalls," Jill said. "Look at Chaplin. And Chevy Chase."

"I don't really know if I want to end up like Chaplin," Toni said. "I'd hate having cream pies in my face. I'd like to end up as a serious actress, I think. I mean, comedy is fun, but it's not real acting, is it? Brandt says they're doing this tense drama next. That will give me a chance to show I can do more than fall off chairs."

"I don't see why you'd want to do more," Jill said. "You're good at making people laugh, Toni. That's a wonderful talent!"

"Maybe," Toni said hesitantly. "But I don't know if I want to be famous as the greatest klutz in the world!" She slid from her stool and wriggled into her jeans. "I hope Brandt can get away from all the bigwigs out front," she said. "What did you think of him, Jill?"

"Very nice," Jill said. "He seems just right for you."

Toni grinned from ear to ear. "He really is. He's wonderful . . . and so grown-up. To think that I've wasted my time with little boys until now when there were people like Brandt waiting out there."

"You were a little girl until fairly recently," Jill reminded her.

"I was not," Toni said, buttoning her blouse quickly. "I was always exceptionally mature for my age. You had no idea how much I was suffering, stuck among you children in high school."

"Okay, grandma," Jill said, laughing. "But before we go maybe you ought to let me button your blouse for you properly—you missed the top button, and it's all uneven."

"Very funny." Toni frowned at herself in the mirror as Jill chuckled and started to rearrange the buttons. "Just because I flunked blouse buttoning in kindergarten because I was to busy learning about life—"

She swept a brush through her tangled hair once more and hastily applied some ordinary makeup. "This feels good after the greasepaint. I hate the way that feels on my skin," she said. "But I suppose I'll have to get used to it if I want to be a star someday. Come on, let's go see who's waiting for me." And she swept down the hall ahead of Jill.

A group of people had gathered at the side entrance waiting. "There she is, there's the star!" somebody called and everyone moved toward Toni. Soon she was being swept along on a tide of people, leaving Jill stranded behind her.

THIRTEEN

"Hey, listen to this one," Toni said, looking up from her newspaper. "'Toni Redmond sparkled with champagne wit . . .' That's pretty classy, isn't it?"

"Very classy," Jill said. "Was that the reporter with the bald head that you poured the champagne over? Maybe that's what made champagne stick in his head."

"You're mean," Toni said, wrinkling her nose. "And I didn't pour champagne over his head. He bent down to pick up his pen and came up under my glass of champagne."

"Sure," Jill said.

It was late the next morning. Jill and Toni had arrived back at Toni's apartment just before dawn. Toni had offered Jill her bed, but Jill had insisted on bedding down on two floor pillows.

"You're the star, not me," she'd said.

"Okay, but you'll probably be sorry in the morning." Toni had warned.

ON OUR OWN

When Toni had jumped out of bed feeling as bright and bubbly as she'd felt the night before, Jill had smiled wanly and admitted Toni had been right. "Those two pillows kept sliding apart, so part of me spent half the night on the cold floorboards. And I have a splitting headache," Jill had added, "even though I didn't drink any champagne."

"You'll feel better after you eat something—and after you read my reviews." Toni had been dressing while she talked. "I'll be right back. If any agents call while I'm gone, tell them *I'll* call *them*," she'd called over her shoulder as she'd strutted out the door.

When Toni had returned—her arms filled with newspapers, plus a bag of croissants, Jill had had a pot of coffee ready. They had devoured the croissants, strawberry jam, and coffee while Toni scanned the newspapers for the reviews of her play. Now, curled on her bed, surrounded by newspapers, Toni was rereading the reviews aloud to Jill. They were all good. They all made special mention of Toni.

"That's the last one," Toni said, lying back and letting the paper slip to the floor. "Wasn't that a lovely party last night?" she asked. "Wasn't it one of the loveliest parties you've ever been to? Everything elegant. No crummy little high school or college kids making juvenile jokes . . . And most of the people who were there are rich—very rich . . . Did you hear them comparing my play with plays they'd seen in London and New York? . . . They all thought I was wonderful . . . adorable . . . cute . . . clever . . . you heard them, Jill.

"Yes . . . I did," Jill answered. "I thought most of them sounded a bit phony—"

"Phony!" Toni sat up. "That was the real world, Jill," she said emphatically. "The world I want to belong to. Brandt always says that you should reach out and seize the moment, and this is my moment." She sat up suddenly and looked across at Jill. "Don't you think so? Tell me honestly, what do *you* think I should do now?"

"Do now?" Jill asked, looking baffled. "You mean go out somewhere?"

Toni laughed. "No, dummy. I mean with my life—my career. I don't want to take a wrong turn, do I? I have to plan it out very carefully."

"But you haven't even finished your first year of college yet," Jill said. "You have that to get through before you can make any more plans."

"College!" Toni said in a crushing voice. "Community college—big deal! Frankly I've had enough community college to last me a lifetime. Those people are so juvenile and boring, and I'm not learning anything useful at all. I mean, who needs business math and computers. I suppose they're fine if you only want to wind up in an office, making coffee for the boss, but not for me—no sirree!"

"You mean you're thinking of dropping out?" Jill asked, horrified.

"Why not?" Toni replied sharply. "I've proved I can make it in the theater, haven't I? The big decision I have to make is whether I try Hollywood first or head straight for Broadway. It's hard to know. Movies and TV do pay well, but they don't really have the prestige of the theater, do they?"

Jill stared at her friend. "Hey, hold on a minute," she said. "Aren't you jumping the gun a little bit? You've only been in one play—one night of one play, to be exact. You were very good, I agree, but that still doesn't make you a professional actress overnight. You have to study to be an actress, just like everything else."

"Brandt doesn't really think so," Toni said. "He thinks that a lot of natural talent gets stifled by formal training."

"But you can't just go charging off to Hollywood, Toni," Jill said. "Nobody makes it as an actress right away. You need some skills to fall back on. Even that business math might come in handy."

"I have skills," Toni said. "You should see me being efficient in that office. . . . Of course, that'll all be different from now on. If I decide to stay awhile, they won't have the nerve to order me around again. They'll probably offer to make *me* coffee from now on!"

Jill looked at Toni uneasily. "So you're heading straight for Hollywood?" she asked.

"Maybe not *straight*," Toni said. "I might stick around until the end of the year. I don't want to leave Brandt right now, and I think the play he's going to be doing next will be good for my career. I'd like to do a meaty drama after this little mermaid thing, and it'll show everyone I can really act. You wait until you see that play, Jill. Belinda is so evil—so wonderfully cold and calculating. She destroys a whole family, one by one. I can't wait!"

"I can't imagine you being evil, cold, and calculating," Jill said, studying her friend hard.

"You wait until you see the play," Toni said. "When I have a whole pile of reviews from it—I can head wherever I want. Isn't it exciting—it's all happening, Jill! Suddenly life is opening up in front of me!" She got up and began to sing, "Things look swell, things look great!"

"Quiet up-a there," came a booming voice from downstairs. Toni sighed and glared at the floorboards. "This apartment will be the first thing to go when I'm famous," she said. "In fact I think I'll ditch Seattle altogether. Perhaps I can get Brandt to come back to L.A. with me. He's wasted up here, and he doesn't really like it, anyway. We'll get a little apartment right off Sunset Boulevard, with a pool and palm trees . . ."

"Has it gotten to the stage of you two talking about getting an apartment together?" Jill asked with surprise.

Toni grinned. "Not exactly," she said. "But it will. Especially if I'm going to be a star. Everyone likes to latch onto a star. I'll let him direct my pictures. He's a wonderful director, Jill. He knows exactly what he wants, and he can explain things so well. In fact, he's the most perfect person for me. I'm so happy I could shout it right out the window."

"If you do that they'll send for the cops," Jill said. "But I do agree that Brandt is really nice. And a good director. Anyone who can get you through a whole play without destroying the set has got to have something going for him."

"Thanks a lot," Toni said, hurling a pillow at Jill. "And speaking of boyfriends . . . Where was Craig, I'd like to know. What was so important that he missed my opening night?

Jill shrugged her shoulders. "I didn't invite him," she said.

"You didn't invite him—how come?" Toni demanded.

"Because I thought it might be embarrassing," Jill said, looking down at her hands. "Things aren't going too well with us."

"You mean you're breaking up?"

"I hope not, but I don't know. I don't want to go on like this—in a way I'd rather break up than just keep drifting apart, and that's what seems to be happening right now. He's so caught up in his own life, he just doesn't have time for me. Every time I call him, he's busy or something . . ."

"And what happened that weekend when you were both home?" Toni asked. "Didn't you get some time together then?"

"That was the most scary thing of all, Toni," Jill said, playing with the fringe around the pillow, braiding it and unbraiding it as she spoke. "We didn't know what to say to each other. We were polite. There were long silences. I felt as if I were talking to a stranger. He asked me if I'd met somebody else and I told him I hadn't. Then he said that he wanted me to feel free—that neither of us should consider ourselves trapped or tied down. I got the impression that he was the one who was feeling trapped and that he might even have someone else waiting back at college!"

"The rat," Toni said angrily. "After all you've done for him. You came rushing back from Italy just because he felt lonely!"

Jill smiled. "I'm not blaming him, Toni. People do change a lot at our age. Maybe we're just outgrowing each other—maybe our interests and our friends are too different . . ."

"I always thought you were getting much too serious," Toni said. "I was worried you'd end up with two point one kids and a station wagon, just like your sister. This could be the best thing that ever happened to you!"

"It doesn't feel like the best thing," Jill said miserably. "I don't really know what to do next."

"That's obvious—date other guys. Go to parties. Have a great time."

Jill sighed. "That's the trouble. I don't want to date other guys. Every one I meet, I find myself comparing him to Craig. I don't know if I'll ever be able to get him out of my mind."

"When you meet someone who's cute enough, you will," Toni said, giving Jill a teasing grin. "Like me when I saw Brandt. You've got to learn to live, Jill Gardner! Just as I intend to. No more boring old college classes. No more making coffee and filing. No more living on frozen macaroni and cheese. Everything's going to be beautiful . . .".

"Hey, no more choruses from *Gypsy*," Jill warned. "We don't want that old guy downstairs thumping on the ceiling again!"

"I'm sorry, but I'm so happy, Jill, and I want you to be happy, too," Toni said. "I realize that college is full of juvenile little kids, but there have to be some cute older guys at Rosemont. Maybe I'll come down one of these days and select one for you . . ."

"You'd better not, Toni Redmond," Jill said severely. "You just concentrate on being a star and leave Rosemont to me."

"Maybe I could come down in a touring company some time," Toni said. "Don't they have a Shakespeare festival in the spring? I can just see myself as Lady Macbeth or Ophelia!" She grabbed the bedspread to drape around herself. "Out, damned spot! Out, I say!" she quoted, striding across the room. Unfortunately the remains of her breakfast were still on the bedspread. The plate fell to the floor and shattered. The knife and fork landed on top of it with a clatter.

"What's-a going on up-a there?" came a booming voice from downstairs.

"Earthquake, Mr. Paolini!" Toni yelled back.

Jill lay back, laughing helplessly. "One thing about you, Toni Redmond," she said at last. "Being with you is never dull!"

FOURTEEN

The play ran for two more weekends to sellout crowds. People around college started to recognize Toni and say nice things to her.

"I heard you were a big success in your play," Bill, her computer teacher, said one day as she was leaving his classroom.

"You mean you didn't even see me?" Toni asked, grinning at him.

"I don't usually go in for light comedy," he said. "Serious theater is more my style."

"Then you have to come to our next production," she said. "*A Walk in the Dark*—do you know it?"

"I think so," he said. "Is that the one with the old southern family and the horrible bride?"

"That's it," Toni said. "I'm going to play the horrible bride."

Bill looked surprised. "But I always think of you as such a sweet young thing," he said, laughing. "I don't know if I want to come and watch you drive people to suicide."

"Good actresses can play any part," Toni said. "That's what I have to prove to people now—that I can do more than just comedy."

"You sound serious about it," he said. "So does that mean you'll be switching to acting classes, just when I thought you were getting the hang of computers?"

"I may be switching to no classes at all," Toni said. "If this all goes well, I'll probably go to New York after New Year's. I really need professional experience right now."

"It's your life," Bill said, shrugging his shoulders. "But it seems to me that everyone these days is smart to go to college first."

"Only if you want to end up in a boring old job," Toni said. "I intend to spread my wings and fly!"

He shook his head and laughed. "I hope you have practiced happy landings," he said, turning to walk away.

Her business math teacher, Mrs. Barton, was not as pleasant. She stopped Toni as she was leaving her classroom. "Toni—you and I have to talk about that last test," she said. "Your mark was terrible. I had the feeling you didn't understand any of the questions."

"I would have understood them if someone had explained them properly," Toni said coldly.

"The rest of the class seems to understand," Mrs. Barton said.

"The rest of the class has probably been studying business math for the past fifty-five years," Toni said. "So I flunked one test. It's no big deal."

"If you want a passing grade in this class you will have to retake the test," Mrs. Barton said icily.

Toni gave her famous withering stare. "Frankly, Mrs. Barton, I don't give a damn," she said and swept off down the hall, grinning to herself as soon as she was out of sight.

What does it matter what that stupid old witch thinks, she told herself. *I'm never going to need her dumb business math. Let her go ahead and fail me! This college is getting more and more on my nerves every minute. I don't think I'll bother to finish up this quarter. I might as well quit right now.*

She sat on a bench in the courtyard, watching the students hurry past to classes. "Look at them," she muttered to herself. "Every one of them is boring and juvenile. I don't belong here."

"Hey, Toni!" Dina yelled, running down the steps, accompanied by a group of boys. "Where have you been? We never see you these days!"

"I've been pretty busy acting in the play," Toni said.

"The college play?" Dina asked, surprised.

"No, dummy, she was in some real theater downtown," one of the boys with Dina said. "She's a famous person, didn't you know that?"

"No, I didn't know," Dina said, looking at Toni as if she'd only just noticed her for the first time. "No kidding, Toni?"

Toni shrugged her shoulders. "I played the mermaid in the Theater Alliance play."

"Wow," Dina said, "I know a celebrity—how about that? You should try out for the next college play. They put on great productions here—have you seen any of them? I'll bet you could get a part."

"Er, thanks but no thanks," Toni said. "I've got my acting work lined up for the next few months. One more production at the Theater Alliance and then I'll probably be joining a fully professional company."

"Wow," Dina said again. "Isn't she something?"

"Hey, miss, can I have your autograph?" one of the boys asked, laughing.

"Hey, miss, can I have a date with you?" another asked. "I've never had a date with a famous person!" The two boys nudged each other and started chuckling.

"You guys are so crude," the third boy said. He sat down beside Toni. "Hey, baby," he said. "I get the feeling you and I were meant for each other. I'm Taurus. What's your sign?"

Toni gave him a crushing look. "No dogs allowed," she said and got to her feet, walking through the group of laughing kids and away across the steps.

At work that day Toni had to send out a press notice for tryouts for *A Walk in the Dark*.

"Do I have to come and try out with everyone else?" she asked Brandt, who had come up with the notice.

"I didn't know you wanted to try out," he said, surprised.

"You bet. I'm going to be Belinda," Toni said. "Don't I get a private audition from the director?"

Brandt laughed and took her into his arms. "You get plenty of private time with me," he said. "But if you want to try out for one of my plays, you show up with everyone else."

"I thought mermaids got special privileges," Toni quipped.

Brandt looked down at her, suddenly serious. "No special privileges, Toni," he said. "If you're the best person, you'll get the part, but don't count on me for favors. If I want to build up my reputation as a director, I can't be the kind of guy who slips his girlfriend into the best parts, can I?"

"You won't have to slip me in anywhere," Toni said haughtily. "I'll get the part because I'm the best one."

"That's my girl," Brandt said, hugging her to him. "You'll get what you want from life, Toni, because you're a fighter."

That's me—a fighter, Toni thought late the following afternoon as she studied her lines for the audition. *Belinda is a fighter, too, but she's much more*

underhanded. I've got to practice being subtle and evil.
She looked at herself in the mirror, giving her best
evil glance. "No, that's wrong," she said aloud,
laughing at herself. "That's too much like the wicked
women in soap operas. Belinda has to be innocent
and evil at the same time: 'But you won't leave, will
you Rodney? You can't leave me even if you want
to. . . . Sit down, Rodney, there's a good boy. You
see, you still do what I tell you to!'"

"Toni, are you in there. . . . Is something the
matter?" Chris the fisherman called, knocking on
her half-open door.

Toni looked up and blushed. "I was just reading
lines for the next play," she said, grinning. "I didn't
realize my door was open."

"Oh, that's all right, then," Chris said, pushing
his hair back under his cap. "I thought you'd flipped
or something. You must tell us when the play is
going to be on. We really thought you were terrific
as the mermaid . . . being specialists in mermaids,
that is."

"You wait till you see me drive poor Rodney to
shoot himself," Toni said, giving her evil smile.

"You'd better make sure your door is closed or
old Mrs. Hansen might have a heart attack if she
hears you acting like that." He gave a friendly wave,
and Toni went back to the play. She worked
nonstop, going over and over any scene that might
be used for tryouts. By the time she left for the

theater she was feeling confident that she knew Belinda well.

Among those waiting to audition when Toni arrived, were several other young actresses, obviously trying out for the part of Belinda. They perched uneasily on the edge of their seats, some staring straight ahead, some buried in their scripts.

They look like a pretty wimpy bunch, Toni decided. *Not much competition there.*

"Didn't you play the mermaid in the last production?" one of them asked.

Toni admitted that she had.

"You were really good," the girl said, looking envious. "Everybody in the audience laughed so much."

"Are you trying out for Belinda, too?" another girl asked. "I heard they might use professional actors to play the leads."

"Brandt—the director—said he might bring someone up from L.A. to play Big Daddy," Toni confided. "I guess anyone has a chance for Belinda."

"Not with you here," the first girl said. "I don't know why I bothered to come, really, except that I've always loved this play, and Belinda is the only young woman's part."

Then the door opened and, one by one, they were called through into the theater. Toni was called last. That alone gave her extra confidence. *They want to see how the others measure up to me*, she told herself.

When her turn came she strode confidently onto the stage she already knew well. Everything was so familiar . . .

"Okay, Toni," Brandt's voice came from the auditorium. "Act Two, Scene Three. The scene with Rodney in the bedroom. Tom here will read Rodney." A slim young man dressed in a dark turtleneck came onto the stage and pulled up a chair. "This is for your dressing table," he said. "You're sitting, looking in the mirror when I come in."

Toni hardly had to look at her book as she did the scene. She brushed out her hair and laughed as Rodney broke down. She could feel the power and evil of Belinda flowing through the theater. She said her final line and swept out leaving Rodney with his head in his hands.

"Thanks, Toni, that was fine," Brandt said. "Come on down and watch the tryouts for Mama Jean with me." Toni slipped into a seat beside Brandt and squeezed her arm through his. He turned and gave her a quick peck on the cheek before the first older woman came onstage.

Some of the people trying out were very amateurish and rather funny to watch. Some of them were very professional and very good.

This is going to be fun, Toni thought as the evening progressed. *Working with all these people. They're first-class actors.*

When the last person had gone, Brandt got stiffly to his feet. "If I hear another woman saying, 'But, Daddy, honey, think of your heart condition!' I'll scream," he said. "Come on, let's go out for something to eat."

He took Toni's hand and led her out of the theater. "Some of them were so bad, weren't they?" he asked, as they walked across to his car. "That woman with the purple flowers . . . I had to keep looking down at my script so that she didn't see me laughing."

"But there were some good ones, too," Toni said. "The lady in red. She could really act."

"That's Charlene," he said. "She's a pro. I wanted her all along, but this theater company insists on open auditions, so I have to sit through painful hours of listening to ladies who love the idea of being an actress, but who never bothered to learn how to act."

"What about Belinda" Toni asked cautiously. "Did you get all terrible people trying out for her part?"

"No, there were some good Belindas," he said after a pause. "Some very good Belindas, as a matter of fact." He took Toni's hand. "Look, Toni, would it mean very much to you, if you didn't get the part?"

Toni spun to face him. "What are you talking about?" she said in a scared voice. "Of course I want to get the part. I did fine in the tryouts, didn't I?"

"Yes, sure, you did fine," he said. "You read the lines very well." He stopped and took both her hands in his. "Look, Toni—I didn't want to talk about this until morning because I have a feeling you're going to jump down my throat . . . but I have to say it now: I'm not giving you the part."

"You're not?" Toni's voice quavered. "Why not?"

"You're just not right for it, Toni."

"But I thought I was pretty good," Toni said. Suddenly she felt very hot and clammy, even though the wind was whipping in from the Sound.

"You were as good as you could be," Brandt said. "You tried really hard and you're a good actress, but you're not right for Belinda."

"What's wrong with me?" Toni demanded. "You thought I was a good enough actress when I saved your stupid play for you. The critics all thought so, too. Everyone did."

"Toni—you were terrific in that play," Brandt said. "Nobody would deny that. You were funny and warm and witty—just perfect. But, you see, basically you were playing yourself. You're that kind of person—the kind who wisecracks and falls off chairs and makes men fall in love with you. But you're not Belinda. When you read those lines, I saw Toni, pretending to be Belinda, that's all."

"But I could get into the part, I know I could," Toni pleaded. "How can you judge when I was just reading lines from a book?"

ON OUR OWN

Brandt squeezed her hands. "Toni, you're just not mature enough yet. You have a lot of raw talent, I can see that, but raw talent isn't enough for a part like this. You still come across as a young girl, not a wicked woman with a whole lot of experience of the world. Maybe, when you've been through acting classes, you'll be able to play parts like this, but you've got a lot of growing up to do first."

Toni felt tears welling up in her eyes. She fought them back. She wasn't going to let Brandt see her cry. Nobody was going to see her cry.

"You seemed to find me mature enough," she said bitterly. "Or do you like going around with immature little girls?"

Brandt gave a half laugh. "My private life has nothing to do with this, Toni," he said. "What I feel about you as a person has nothing to do with which actress I choose for a part!"

"It has everything to do with it," Toni said angrily. "I saw those wimpy girls trying out with me. I bet none of them was any better than I was. You just didn't want anyone to accuse you of playing favorites with your girlfriend. Well, if you don't think I'm mature enough, maybe I'd better go find myself a boy of my own age and leave the older women to you." She wrenched herself free of his hands and started to run down the street.

"Toni—now wait a minute," he called after her.

"Just leave me alone," she shouted as she ran. "Go back to your precious play. I don't ever want to see you again."

152

FIFTEEN

The apartment was icy cold when Toni let herself in. She'd run most of the way home and she'd been sweating. Now she began to shiver uncontrollably. She turned on the light and stood in the doorway. The light flickered, faded, and came on again. In that unreal light she was suddenly conscious of the ugliness of the room—the cracks in the wall, the peeling wallpaper, the hole in the rug. Even the new furnishings her parents had made for her—the yellow drapes and the long, low book-shelf—didn't manage to make the room look any better at that moment. It seemed bleak and un-friendly, as if reminding her that she had nowhere to go. She couldn't help thinking about her parents' home—the warmth of the central heating that greeted you as you opened the front door, the thick carpet, and the rooms furnished with her mother's artistic taste. She had a sudden longing to go there now, to say, "Here I am. I'm home. Please take care of me again."

She had even pulled out her overnight bag from behind the sofa bed before her pride surfaced again. "What are you doing, Toni Redmond?" she said aloud severely. "You're not crawling back there the first time things go wrong. You will not give them the chance to say, 'We told you so. We knew it was only a matter of time before you realized that you were better off with us.'" Toni flung the bag back behind the sofa and walked to the kitchen. She turned on the stove and put some water on to boil for coffee. "I'll feel better when I've got something warm in my stomach," she decided, still talking out loud. "It's not the end of the world, after all. I'm not the only person who hasn't gotten a part she wanted. Anyway, it's their bad luck. I'll bet they find out that the other girl is just terrible and then they'll be sorry. Brandt will come crawling back and beg me to take over, just as I took over as the mermaid. Only this time I won't help him out. I'll be busy doing other things, getting on with my own life!"

The water in the pan started to bubble. Toni spooned instant coffee into a mug, poured the boiling water onto it, and moved toward the sofa. She cradled her hands around the mug to warm them, then switched on the small electric heater and crouched beside it. As she sipped the steaming liquid, warmth began to creep back into her body. *There, that's better,* she thought. *Now I'll show Brandt that I don't need him or his crummy, second-rate theater. I'll finish up this quarter of college and then . . .*

Her thoughts were wiped out by a picture of college suddenly coming vividly into her mind. She remembered her conversation with the business math teacher all too clearly and the way her computer professor had been impressed that she was going to play the lead in such a difficult play. How could she ever face them again? "Fine," she said out loud. "So I won't go back to those classes. I couldn't do well in them, anyway. I'll get into classes I like next quarter and make lots of new friends to hang around with . . ." She got up and began pacing up and down the room. "But I've got to pass English," she told herself firmly. "English is a requirement before I can do anything else . . . but that's easy. I can do well in English. No sweat. I'd better finish that term paper after all."

She went over to her desk and rummaged through the pile of papers on top of it. The half-finished term paper was somewhere in the middle, where she'd thrown it after deciding that she was going to quit college. It was now rather crumpled, and Toni tried to smooth out the first two pages between a couple of heavy books. "Only two pages—I thought I'd done more than that," she muttered, picking up her books and her notes from the mess on her desk. "And it must be due pretty soon." She began to read through her notes and gasped. "It's due tomorrow!" she groaned. "Suddenly everything in my life is going wrong at once. How can I possibly finish it by tomorrow morning? I'll be up all night."

She pulled her chair up to the desk and sat down with a sigh, pushing papers onto the floor to give herself some space. *Maybe it's not as much work as it seems*, she thought hopefully. *Maybe once I get started the ideas will come flooding out and I'll write pages and pages and they'll think I'm a genius . . .*

She looked down at a half-finished sentence and sucked at her pen. *If only Jill were here*, she thought. Words came so easily to Jill. She would have taken one look at the title and told Toni exactly what quotes she needed and how she could develop her thesis.

"That's it," Toni shouted, leaping up and letting the book on her lap fall to the floor. "I'll call Jill. She'll be able to tell me what to write." Suddenly she felt a tiny bit hopeful, as if just talking to Jill, hearing her voice, would make things right again. Jill would understand how she felt about not getting the part. Jill had always come through for her in a crisis. She knew just what to say to cheer Toni up. Toni rummaged in her purse and brought out two dimes. "Come on," she growled angrily. "there's got to be more change than that." She spilled everything onto the bed, going through her makeup, her diary, her wallet. But the search only turned up three pennies. She ran across the hall and knocked on the fishermen's door, but nobody was home.

"Rats," she muttered, going back into her room again and fighting back tears of disappointment. She sat back at her desk and frowned down at the paper. "Okay, let's get this straight," she said to the world in general. "I am going to finish this paper whatever happens."

At that moment the lights flickered again and went out. In the darkened house below her she could hear yells and cries: "Mr. Paolini—what happened to the electricity?" "Get these lights back on again!" "My stove's gone out and I'm in the middle of cooking dinner!" and Paolini's booming voice, "Don't-a panic. Don't-a panic, folks. I'm on-a my way down to the basement to see what I can-a do. Just a fuse blow, I bet."

"Fuse, my aunt Fanny," a sharp female voice shouted—that would be the weird librarian on the ground floor. "The wiring in this house is in shreds, Paolini. It's a disgrace. I'm going to call the fire department before the whole place burns down."

Toni sat, not moving, in the darkness. The street lamp outside threw eerie tree shadows across her wall and outlined her furniture, but it was too dark to see anything clearly. Toni suddenly felt like a balloon that had finally popped. She'd been hurt and disappointed and she'd tried to go on, but suddenly she knew that she couldn't.

"It's no good," she said, getting unsteadily to her feet, then leaning back over to unplug the now-useless electric heater. "I can't go back to college and face all those people. I can't face Brandt and the women in the office. I've got to get away from here right now before anything else goes wrong."

She grabbed her jacket and ran out, slamming the door behind her.

SIXTEEN

At Rosemont College, Jill opened the door of her closet, stepped back with a little scream.

"Surprise!" Toni said weakly.

"Toni Redmond, have you gone out of your mind?" Jill shrieked. "Do you realized you almost gave me a heart attack? If this is your idea of a fun trick to play on a friend . . . then I don't think it's very funny." She sank back on her bed, still breathing heavily. "What were you doing in my closet?" she demanded.

"You weren't here when I got here so I thought I'd hide in case your roommate came in," Toni said. "I didn't want to talk to her. I just wanted to see you."

"Did it occur to you that Cassie might have keeled over, too, if she'd opened the closet door and seen a face a few inches from hers?" Jill asked, shaking her head in disbelief. "Why didn't you want to see Cassie, anyway?"

"I don't want to talk to anyone," Toni said. "I don't feel like talking to people."

Jill laughed uneasily. "You came all the way down here to tell me you don't want to talk to people?" she asked.

Toni walked across the room and sat on the other bed. "I'm running away," she said.

"Oh, what from?" Jill asked.

"From me, I guess," Toni said after a long pause.

"Then I don't think you'll make it," Jill said, giving her friend a little smile. "You want to talk about it, or shall I make you some coffee?"

"Coffee, please," Toni said quietly. "I'm so cold. I came down on the early Greyhound and I've been walking around since five A.M., waiting for you and all the other Rosemonters to wake up. I guess I waited too long. Where were you? I expected to find you in bed."

"Having breakfast," Jill said and went over to her desk to plug in the electric pot. She took out two mugs and put instant coffee in both of them, then two huge spoons of sugar into one. Neither girl spoke as the water began bubbling and Jill poured it into the mugs. "Here," she said, handing the one with sugar to Toni. "Sorry there's no milk. We drank it all last night. I can find some nondairy creamer if you'd like."

"This will do fine," Toni said, taking a sip. "It's good and hot. Besides, I never did like nondairy creamer. How can you pretend coconuts are milk? And it's not fair to cows, after all their hard work."

160

Jill grinned. "Oh Toni, what's gone wrong this time?" she asked. "Everything seemed to be turning out so wonderfully for you when I was up for the play. You were a success in the play, weren't you?"

Toni nodded.

"And still going with Brandt?"

Toni nodded again.

"And getting a lot of respect in the office?"

Toni nodded.

"So what can possibly be the matter? Is it something terrible? Something you can't tell anyone else about?"

Toni nodded again.

"But you want to tell me?"

Toni nodded.

"Toni—would you please say something? I'm getting seasick watching your head bob up and down."

"I'm scared to talk," Toni said at last. "I have a horrible feeling I'm going to cry."

"Then go ahead and cry. You'll feel much better afterward—only tell me what's wrong. I can't stand the suspense much longer."

Toni started winding her hair around her finger, as she always did when she was under stress. "I didn't get that part in the play," she said at last in a small voice.

Jill's eyes opened very wide. "That's it?" she asked, her voice rising to a squeak. "You ran away in the middle of the night because you didn't get a part in a play? Toni—I was expecting the worst. I thought at least you were pregnant or had a terminal disease or were wanted for a heinous crime."

"It's that bad to me," Toni said, her voice quavering. "It feels like the end of the world to me."

Jill got up and went to sit next to her friend. She put an arm around her shoulder. "I know you had big dreams for that play, Toni," she said. "But you're just starting out. There will be lots of parts you won't get—lots of disappointments, if you want to be an actress. You'll get another part soon, I'm sure. You were so good as the mermaid."

"But you don't understand, Jill," Toni said. "I had to get that part. It was a matter of life or death for me."

"Oh, come on, Toni. No part is that important. I'll bet there are tryouts for new plays all the time. What about in your college—they put on plays?"

Toni shuddered. "I can't go back to college, anymore," she said.

"Why not?" Jill sounded horrified.

"Because I told them what I thought of them," Toni said in a small voice. "I told them all that their college was boring and dumb and juvenile and I was quitting to go on to much bigger things."

"Why on earth did you do that?" Jill stammered.

"Because I was so sure I'd get that part. I thought I'd never need to go back there again. I was going to go to Broadway or Hollywood. . . . Oh, Jill,

I made such a fool of myself. That's why I ran away. I can't ever face anyone in Seattle again."

"So what do you plan to do?" Jill asked. "Where will you go?"

Toni shrugged her shoulders. "I thought I might try L.A. Maybe get some bit parts in movies."

"But you don't know anyone in L.A., Toni. What if you don't get parts in movies—how would you pay for an apartment if you can't find a job? You hear terrible stories about what happens to girls who land in big cities with nowhere to go. . . . I don't want anything bad to happen to you."

"I can take care of myself," Toni said. "I'm not that dumb, you know."

"I'm sure you can, but I don't even like to think of you lonely and starving, Toni. Nobody ever achieved anything by running away. And think of your folks. They'll be worried out of their minds. . . . That wouldn't be too good for your father's heart."

Toni looked up suddenly. "Do you think it could bring on another heart attack?" she asked.

"Any big worry can," Jill said.

"Oh," Toni said at last. "I wouldn't want that to happen. But I don't want to go back and face all those people. What should I do, Jill?"

"You could go back to your job—drop out of college until the next quarter, or the one after that, maybe, but keep on working," Jill suggested. "You liked that, didn't you?"

"How can I go back there?" Toni demanded, her voice cracking. "Imagine sitting in that office every day, knowing that downstairs some other girl is acting my part. And the women in the office—they'd look at one another and say, 'She was only good for one part—now she's back to being an office girl again.'"

"I'm sure they're not as bitchy as that," Jill said. "Unless you acted like a big shot around them . . ."

Toni's face flushed red. "I guess I did, a little bit," she said. "It was so nice to be treated like a star . . ."

"And what about Brandt?" Jill asked. "You're breaking up with him, too?"

"That double-crossing creep?" Toni asked. "What a jerk. To think I was actually in love with him, Jill. How could he say that I was special to him and then choose someone else for my part?"

"But, Toni, he wasn't giving the part to his favorite person. He was giving it to the person who could do it best."

"That's what he said, the nasty, horrible jerk."

"So I take it you've broken up with him?" Jill asked.

"I walked away and told him I never wanted to see him again," Toni said.

"And don't you?"

"How can I, Jill? How can I ever forget that he let me down? How could I go to rehearsals with him and watch him directing someone else?"

"I get the impression that you still care about him."

"I was crazy about him. You know that. But he's hurt me, Jill. I can't get over that. I don't want to see him again."

"I think you're making a bit mistake, Toni," Jill said kindly. "From what I hear, you two still care about each other. He's just acting like a professional director. He's just doing his job, Toni. If he didn't think you were right for the part, then it would ruin his career to give it to you. You wouldn't want that, would you? You know how people are—if you acted the part badly, everyone would whisper behind your backs, 'We all know why she got the part, don't we?' and think how you'd feel then. Maybe the director of the company—Mrs. Thompson—would hear the whispers and fire him. Is that what you want?"

Toni shook her head. "I guess not," she said.

"You said yourself that he was a great director," Jill said. "It can't have been easy for him to turn you down for the part, so he really must have had someone better in mind."

"The other girls all seemed so wimpy," Toni said hesitantly, "but someone did say something about bringing in professionals for the leads. Maybe he had a real actress in mind for the part . . ." She sank back and gave a big sigh. "I was so sure I was doing it well, Jill. But all the way down here on that bus I went over the lines in my head and they sounded like good old Toni, not like an evil woman. Maybe I'm not an actress after all. . . . I only got that last part because I was a klutz who happened to look right . . ."

Jill put her hand on Toni's arm. "Maybe you did," she said. "That's how lots of people get chosen for parts—because they fit the role. But what they do with the part is up to the person. You made everyone fall off their seats laughing, Toni. They stood up and applauded you, so how could you think you didn't do a great job? You'd probably do a great job with the wicked woman in a few years' time—you just aren't old enough yet, and you haven't been trained for serious acting."

Toni put her hand on Jill's. "You're right," she said. "Maybe I do need training. I know now that there's nothing in the world I want to do except act, so I'd better sign up for some acting classes, right?"

"That's the first sensible thing you've said all morning," Jill said, smiling at her warmly. "This running away just wasn't like you. The Toni Redmond I know never ran away from things. She was a fighter. You just keep on fighting, Toni, because I want a best friend who is a terrific actress by the time I get out of college. I might want you to star in a play I've written."

"Hey, wouldn't that be cool?" Toni asked, looking hopeful for the first time. "Only you'd better write a play with a sexy leading lady in it. I don't want to play anyone wimpy."

Jill glanced at her watch. "Look, Toni," she said, "stay as long as you want to, but I have to get to morning classes. My English professor does not accept excuses for lateness, even if I claimed heart failure after finding a person in my closet. If you're still around by lunchtime, we'll eat together and you can see how much the cafeteria food has improved. . . . But if you want my advice, I'd go straight back and behave as if nothing is different. I'd go to my office and do a good day's work. Then they'll really respect you, because they knew how much the play meant to you. I'd also go and talk to Brandt . . ."

"Maybe," Toni said hesitantly.

Just then there was a tapping on the window. Toni looked up to see a tall, lanky boy with a lot of sandy hair waving frantically at Jill.

Jill walked across and pushed up the window. "You go ahead, Robert," she said. "I've got my friend Toni visiting from Seattle. Toni, this is Robert—Robert—Toni. I'll come as soon as I can. Cover for me if Dr. Holloman asks where I am."

"Okay, Jill," he said. "But I don't think I do a very good imitation of you—could you lend me your sweater, maybe?"

He and Jill both started laughing. "You looked very sweet in it," Jill said, watching Robert's cheeks turn pink. She turned to Toni. "He was cold on a hike we took, so I lent him my spare sweater. The only trouble was, it was pink with hearts on it."

"Listen, it was better than freezing to death," Robert said. "But only just! I'll get going then, Jill. Nice to meet you—Toni."

"He seems very nice," Toni said as Robert bounded away across the lawn.

"He is." Jill smiled. "I'm glad I have him in my English class. The rest of the students are so serious."

"He seems pretty interested in you," Toni said thoughtfully.

Jill flushed a little. "He is," she said.

"Have you gone out with him?"

"How can I?" Jill said. "You know how I feel about Craig—and it wouldn't be fair to Robert to let him think I considered him anything more than a friend."

"For heaven's sake," Toni said. "I'm not suggesting that you get married or start living together. It sounds as though Craig wants to date other people. Maybe you should try it, too. You can't sit here like a hermit for four years, just hoping Craig still wants you as his girl at the end of it."

"I know, but . . ." Jill began.

"No buts," Toni said. "You were very depressed last time I talked to you. If being with Craig doesn't make you happy anymore, then it's time you moved on. Just go out with someone like Robert, as friends. Who knows, maybe it will lead to something more, maybe it won't. Anyway, you'll have a good time and you'll get back into the swing of dating again. If you're not careful I'll run after Robert and tell him to ask you out."

"Don't you dare," Jill said, looking alarmed. "But, as a matter of fact, he did ask me if I wanted to come to the foreign film festival they're having on campus."

"Well, there you are," Toni said. "Perfect first date. Go for it."

"You make it sound so easy," Jill said.

"It is," Toni said. "You've got to learn. We're not in high school now. We don't have to go steady any time a guy takes us to a movie. We're free to make lots of new friends, both boys and girls. Next time I talk to you, I want to hear that you've been dating guys . . . and that's an order."

Jill smiled. "We'll see," she said. "I do feel comfortable with Robert, it's just that he doesn't send tingles up my spine."

"But that would be terrible," Toni said. "Just think how it would be if every guy we met sent tingles all over us—like living in the middle of a switchboard!"

Jill laughed. "If you're so smart," she said, "you can tell me how to get rid of a guy, without hurting his feelings."

"The creepy Charles?" Toni asked. "Is he still hanging around?"

"More than ever," Jill said. "He keeps asking me out to things and I have to invent more and more complicated excuses. Honestly, Toni—I don't think I

169

could stand an evening alone with him. He wanted to take me out to dinner . . ."

"That's easy," Toni said. "Just tell him that you want to go to a Tibetan yak restaurant. He won't be able to find any of those, so you'll be safe!"

Jill laughed. "You're crazy," she said.

Toni's face suddenly got serious again. "I guess I have been pretty crazy for a while," she said. "I've behaved like a jerk to everyone. Do you really think they'll all forgive me and let me start over?"

"I can't guarantee it," Jill said, "but it's worth a try. Everyone knows that being a star goes to people's heads sometimes. You're lucky you've gotten your swelled-head stage over with now. Just think of the consequences if it had happened in acting school or on Broadway. . . . You really could have made enemies then . . ."

"But I've made an enemy of Brandt," Toni said. "He's the only one I really want to forgive me. I'm going right back on the next bus, Jill, and I'm going to make him forgive me if it's the last thing I do."

She walked toward the door. "Thanks for the advice," she said, giving a little smile. "I'm going to take it . . . and if everything goes wrong, I'll have someone else to blame!" She laughed as she ran out the door.

SEVENTEEN

Toni let herself into the theater silently through the tall double doors at the back. She stood in the aisle, just taking in the look and feel and smell of the place—the odor of paint and glue and sawdust from a half-made set, the velvet curtains glowing in the half light, the rows of seats fading into darkness on either side.

I love it, she said to herself. *I love everything about it. There's nowhere else I'd rather be. . . . I don't care how long it takes or how hard I have to work, but someday people are going to come to plays just to see me . . . and when I walk down the street they're going to nudge each other and whisper, "There's goes Toni Redmond, the actress."*

She started to walk forward, letting her hand trail over the soft velvet of the seats on either side of the aisle. Then she noticed that she wasn't alone. Brandt was sitting on a stool in a corner of the stage, under the one small light that was on up there. He had his head deep in a book. He looked so alone that Toni longed to rush up and put her arms around

171

him. But she remembered, all too clearly, how they'd parted. She'd told him she never wanted to see him again. . . . Would he still want to see her after that scene?

She hung back, hardly daring to breathe in case he turned around and noticed her. She'd come into the theater to be alone, to think. All the way home on the bus, she'd planned what she was going to say to Brandt. But when she'd called his apartment, no one answered. So she had walked—walked through dark and deserted streets until she had ended up at the theater. Now she couldn't wait a second longer. She moved forward quickly and started to climb the steps to the stage. Brandt looked up. She watched the startled look and the hint of a smile come to his face.

"Toni!" he exclaimed.

She walked across the stage toward him. "I behaved like a little kid," she said. "I'm sorry. Can you forgive me?"

Brandt stood up. "Toni—where on earth have you been?" he demanded. "I've been worried sick about you. I've called your apartment, your school, your home, and nobody knew where you were. I was scared you were going to do something dumb!"

"I nearly did," Toni said. "I was going to run away. . . . I don't even know where to. Just get far away and start again. Only I stopped off to see my friend Jill on the way. She helped me see a lot of things. One of them was that I was only thinking about myself. I wasn't being fair to you."

Brandt stretched out his arms toward her. "I would have loved to give you that part, Toni, but I had to give it to the person I thought was best."

"I understand that now," Toni said. "I said a lot of dumb things. . . . I guess I've still got a lot of growing up to do."

Brandt took her hands in his. "We all say things we don't mean when we're upset," Brandt said. "Even mature old men like me."

Toni looked up at him and smiled. "I decided that not getting the part was bad enough, but not seeing you again was even worse. Now you know what a terrible temper I've got. You know that I have little-girl tantrums. Do you still want me back, or shall I just walk out of your life right now?"

"You're funny," he said, gazing down tenderly at her. "It's because you're the sort of person you are that I like you. I knew what I was getting into. I knew I couldn't expect a smooth relationship with a girl who calls the cops on me and traps me in elevators and yells at people in restaurants. But I like excitement. I'm willing to take the chance, if you are."

"Oh, Brandt," Toni said, winding her arms around his neck. He bent to kiss her, and for a long while they stood, still as statues, lit with one pale spotlight.

"Come on, let's shut up this place and I'll drive you home," Brandt said at last. "You must be tired after all that running away."

"Exhausted," Toni agreed. "But I'll make you dinner at my place, if you like."

"Sounds good," Brandt said. He took Toni's hand. "You know what," he said, "if you want to do something with the play, I could always use an assistant . . ."

Toni looked up at him and grinned. "No, thanks," she said. "I'm not very good at being humble. I'd always want to keep leaping onto the stage and saying to the actress, 'This is the way it should be done!'"

Brandt laughed. "I don't think you'd have to do that too much," he said. "You should come down and watch Paulette sometime. She's had a lot of experience. You could learn something from her."

"Maybe I will," Toni said. "I know now that I've got a lot to learn. I'm going to sign up for hundreds of theater classes next quarter."

"Don't try and take on too much again," Brandt said. "After all, you've got a whole life ahead of you. Save enough time to enjoy it."

"Oh, I intend to," Toni said, squeezing his hand. "I intend to enjoy every moment of it from now on . . . once I can get out of business math, that is!"

They walked, laughing, hand in hand, out of the theater and down the block to where Brandt's car was parked.

"I must say this apartment looks a lot better than it did the last time I saw it," Brandt said, pausing in the doorway to look around. "Aren't those new drapes? They don't even clash with the wallpaper! And those bookshelves—they don't look as if they'll fall down if someone blows on them."

"You're very rude!" Toni said, stalking ahead of him across the room and into the kitchen. She pulled the curtain closed behind her. "There never was anything wrong with this apartment. Except maybe the freezing cold and the electricity that always goes off at the wrong moment." She poked her head back through the curtain and grinned. "But the new things are nice, aren't they? My folks brought them over last weekend. Dad made the bookshelves, although Mom wouldn't let him do any hammering or sawing. He just pointed to a spot and Mom hammered. I'll bet it was funny to watch. . . . My mother doesn't follow directions too well and . . ." She paused, open-mouthed. "Did you say you called my house looking for me?"

Brandt nodded.

"And you spoke to my parents?"

"To your mother."

"Jeepers!" Toni said, leaping out from behind the curtain and across the room. "I'd better call them right now. My father might've had another heart attack by now worrying about me!" She started rummaging in her purse. "Quick, have you got any change? The phone in the hall downstairs eats coins faster than you can put them in . . . I've only got one quarter."

Brandt walked over and put a hand on her shoulder. "Relax," he said. "I was very careful of what I said to them. I didn't let them know that I was in a real panic. I remembered about your father's heart and just asked casually if they knew where I could get in touch with you because something urgent had come up at the theater. . . . Here, take this." He pulled out a handful of change from his jeans pocket.

Toni took the change and ran down the two flights of stairs to the front hall. Her hands were trembling as she dropped a coin in the slot. The phone rang three times. *Oh, no,* she thought, *he's had a heart attack and they're both at the hospital. It's all my fault. Why don't I ever stop and think before I do things? Now I'll never . . .*

"Hello?"

"Hello, Mom?" Toni's voice quavered noticeably.

"Toni—is that you? Is everything all right, honey? We had a phone call from Brandt today, and he said he couldn't find you anywhere. Where were you?"

"Everything's fine, Mom. I just went to see Jill."

"For the day?"

"I needed someone to talk to. I had some things to think about."

"Is something wrong, Toni?"

"It's nothing, Mom. I just had a problem I needed to sort out."

"You can always talk to us, you know. I understand that you find it hard to live with us right now, but we're only twenty miles away when you need us."

"I know, Mom, but I had to get away suddenly. I had to do a lot of thinking. The bus trip helped as much as Jill did. I've got everything sorted out again, now."

"Well, that's good. Your father will be relieved to know that you're all right. IT'S TONI, ARTHUR. YES, ON THE PHONE NOW. SHE'S FINE. JUST WENT DOWN TO SEE JILL FOR THE DAY." Toni held the phone away from her ear while her mother yelled down the hall. "YES, I'LL TELL HER, ARTHUR. AND LEAVE THAT LAUNDRY ALONE. I CAN DO IT." Her mother lowered her voice again. "Your father is so stubborn, Toni. Now I can't get him to sit still. He sends his love, by the way."

"Send mine back to him," Toni said. "And maybe you shouldn't make him sit still. As long as you treat him like an invalid, he'll be one. He's got a lot of years ahead of him, Mom. You won't want him to spend them in an armchair, do you?"

"Of course not. It's just that he's like you, Toni. He rushes ahead with things without stopping to think of the consequences. You know what I mean, don't you?"

Toni laughed. "I know what you mean," she said. "But you have to admit, people like us are more fun, aren't we?"

"If you like living dangerously," her mother said, laughing, too. "I hope you've let that poor boy Brandt know you're back safely."

"He's upstairs right now, waiting to be fed. I'd better go feed him. I'll come over this weekend, okay?"

"Bring Brandt with you, if he'd like to come."

"Thanks, Mom. See ya. Love you both."

"We love you too, Toni."

Brandt was standing by the window when Toni came back into the room, staring out thoughtfully. "You can see right across Puget Sound from here," he said. "Look at the lights way over there. It's beautiful." He turned back and smiled at her. "Everything okay at home?"

"Everything's fine," she said. "You're invited this weekend. I hope you like low-everything health food, because that's what my father has to eat."

Brandt grinned. "Right now I'd settle for tofu and bean sprouts with cabbage juice. I'm starving!"

"One gourmet dinner coming right up," Toni said. "Here, grab this bag of potato chips and sit down on the good chair. I'll be out in a minute—but no peeking. It makes me nervous when someone watches me cook, and when I'm nervous I mix up salt and sugar!"

"Okay, I won't peek," Brandt said, shaking his head as he smiled, watching her tenderly. "Only hurry up in there. You know how I hate being left alone!"

Much later Brandt leaned back contentedly in the one good chair.

"Toni—that was a delicious meal," he said. "I had no idea you could cook!"

"Oh, there are lots of things you don't know about me yet," Toni said smoothly.

"So I'm learning," Brandt agreed. "That veal in wine sauce, it was excellent. You must show me how you prepare it next time."

"I told you, I get nervous when anyone else is in the kitchen," Toni said. "I'm one of those cooks who needs a lot of space around me."

"Well, you can come over and cook for me anytime," Brandt said. "My kitchen is enormous."

"I'll have to think about that," Toni said. "I don't want you getting too many chauvinistic ideas that women are here to wait on men."

"Well, what else are they good for?" Brandt asked, his eyes teasing hers. She attacked. "No, Toni, don't tickle me . . . Women are just as good as men, okay? Now will you stop tickling me?"

Dear Jill,

Thank you so much for everything. Things have worked out just fine. Brandt was pleased to see me back and the people in the office are being really nice. They haven't once mentioned anything about me trying for that part. And Mrs. Thompson is talking about getting me into a musical theater workshop program at State U. next summer. Doesn't that sound like fun?

Speaking of acting, you would have been proud of the way I handled that old biddy, Mrs. Barton, my business math teacher. I put on my most humble look, and begged her to let me retake the test I had failed. Of course she fell for my act . . . I knew she would. Well, I did retake the test and got a C—not bad for me! Don't get me wrong, I still think business math is boring and stupid, but at least I won't be failing a course my very first quarter of college.

On the way home from Rosemont, I thought a lot about things, and I decided that the one important thing in life is to have someone you can always turn to . . . like you, Jill. As long as there's just one person in your life who you know will always be on your side, then you can face most things. You helped me when my dad was in the hospital, you helped me when I was really depressed in France, and you were probably the only person who could have made me go back to Seattle and face things. Thanks for being there.

Oh, by the way, you'll be surprised to know that Brandt thinks I'm a terrific cook.

No, I did not serve him spaghetti! The only difficulty about preparing the meal was keeping him out of the kitchen, so that he didn't see the Gourmet Frozen Entree boxes the food came out of! Now he wants me to come and cook for him! Help!!! I think I'd better include a cooking course in my schedule next quarter, don't you?

Luv, luv, luv, Toni.

Dear Toni,

I'm so glad things are working out for you. I knew they would. Too much success too soon often goes to a person's head. I think it went to yours a little, but that's fine, because now it will never happen to you again and you can be lovable and humble even when you're a big star! Just remember not to forget your old friend Jill, who helped you start on your road to the top!

And speaking of friends . . . the nice thing about friends is that they help each other. You gave me the confidence I needed to decide to go out with other guys. I did go to that foreign film festival with Robert and I had such a fun evening. It's different in college. You can go out with guys as friends much more easily and not feel that it's a date (with a capital D). Robert is good to have as a friend. He makes me laugh. I don't think I'd want him as any more than that, but it's good to know I can have a good time and not feel guilty about Craig. Maybe I'm ready for a new big romance in my life? I might just have someone in mind, only I don't know if you'd approve of him. He's not really my type, but he sure is attractive. . . . More later.

Love, Jill.

On Our Own

If you enjoyed reading this book, there are many other series published by Bantam Books which you'll love – SWEET DREAMS, SWEET VALLEY HIGH, CAITLIN, WINNERS, COUPLES and SENIORS. With more on the way – KELLY BLAKE, SWEPT AWAY and SWEET VALLEY TWINS – how can you resist!

These books are all available at your local bookshop or newsagent, though should you find any difficulty in obtaining the books you would like, you can order direct from the publisher, at the address below. Also, if you would like to know more about the series, or would simply like to tell us what you think of the series, write to:

Kim Prior,
Sweet Dreams,
Transworld Publishers Ltd.,
61–63 Uxbridge Road,
Ealing,
London W5 5SA.

To order books, please list the title(s) you would like, and send together with a cheque or postal order made payable to TRANSWORLD PUBLISHERS LTD. Please allow the cost of the book(s) plus postage and packing charges as follows:

All orders up to a total of £5.00   50p
All orders in excess of £5.00   Free

Please note that payment must be made in pounds sterling; other currencies are unacceptable.

(The above applies to readers in the UK and Republic of Ireland only)

If you live in Australia or New Zealand, and would like more information about the series, please write to:

Sally Porter,
Sweet Dreams,
Transworld Publishers (Aust) Pty Ltd.,
15–23 Helles Avenue,
Moorebank,
N.S.W. 2170,
AUSTRALIA

Kiri Martin,
Sweet Dreams,
c/o Corgi and Bantam Books New Zealand,
Cnr. Moselle and Waipareira Avenues,
Henderson,
Auckland,
NEW ZEALAND

Don't miss *any* of
Janet Quin-Harkin's books
available from
Bantam:

Sweet Dreams Special:

1. MY SECRET LOVE

Sweet Dreams Romances:

THIS EXCITING NEW SERIES IS ALL ABOUT THE THREE MOST ENVIED,
IMITATED AND ADMIRED GIRLS IN MIDVALE HIGH SCHOOL: STACY HAR-
COURT, GINA DAMONE AND TESS BELDING. THEY ARE WINNERS—GOLDEN
GIRLS AND VARSITY CHEERLEADERS—YET NOT EVEN THEY CAN AVOID
PROBLEMS WITH BOYFRIENDS, PARENTS, AND LIFE.

No. 1 THE GIRL MOST LIKELY

Stacy Harcourt is the captain of the varsity cheerleading squad, but she
wants to break from her rigid, boring image as "Miss Perfect." But in
doing so will she lose the friendship of Gina and Tess and the captainship
of the squad? Or will she realize that maybe her "perfect" life wasn't so
bad after all.

No. 2 THE ALL AMERICAN GIRL

Gina Damone has problems keeping up socially with the other cheerleaders because of her immigrant parents old-world attitudes. But when she
begins dating All-American Dex Grantham his breezy disregard for her
parents' rules makes her question his sincerity.

No. 3 THE GOOD LUCK GIRL

Cute, cuddly Tess Belding is the first student from Midvale's vocational-
technical program ever to make the cheering squad, but she's going to be
benched unless she can pass her French midterm!

WINNERS – available wherever Bantam
paperbacks are sold!

COUPLES

WHAT EVERY GIRL WANTS MOST OF ALL – TO BE PART OF A COUPLE!

BY LINDA A. COONEY

Meet the couples and couples-to-be at Kennedy High School in this thrilling new series – pretty Chris and athletic Ted, popular Phoebe and serious Brad, the dreamy Griffin and cool D.J. Peter, plain Janie and vampy Lauri, sensitive Woody and troubled, troublesome Brenda. Follow them through their first loves, break-ups and crushes – the joys and pitfalls, the attractions and the special moments.

One new title every month!

Available wherever Bantam paperbacks are sold.

Coming Soon . . .

Couples Special Edition
Summer Heat!